BLAZE!

SPANISH GOLD

Ben Boulden

Blaze! Spanish Gold by Ben Boulden
Text Copyright 2017 by Ben Boulden

Series Concept and Characters Copyright 2015 by Stephen Mertz

Cover Design by Livia Reasoner
The Book Place

All rights reserved.
ISBN-13: 978-1977833228
ISBN-10: 1977833225

This is a work of fiction. The characters, incidents, and dialogues are products of the author's imagination and are not to be construed as real.

No part of this book may be used or reproduced in any manner whatsoever without written permission of the publisher, except in the case of brief quotations embodied in critical articles and reviews.

Blaze Western Series

BLAZE!, Stephen Mertz

BLAZE! #2: THE DEADLY GUNS, Robert J. Randisi

BLAZE! #3: BITTER VALLEY, Wayne D. Dundee

BLAZE! #4: SIX-GUN WEDDING, Jackson Lowry

BLAZE! #5: AMBUSHED, Michael Newton

BLAZE! #6: ZOMBIES OVER YONDER, Stephen Mertz

BLAZE! #7: HATCHET MEN, Michael Newton

BLAZE! #8: RIDE HARD, SHOOT FAST, Wayne D. Dundee

BLAZE! #9: A SON OF THE GUN, Stephen Mertz

BLAZE! #10: HELL'S HALF ACRE, Jackson Lowry

BLAZE! #11: BADLANDS, Michael Newton

BLAZE! #12: BLOODY WYOMING, John Hegenberger

BLAZE! #13: NIGHT RIDERS, Michael Newton

BLAZE! #14: THE CHRISTMAS JOURNEY, Stephen Mertz

BLAZE! #15: RED ROCK RAMPAGE, Benjamin Boulden

BLAZE! #16: COPPER MOUNTAIN KILL, Brian Drake

BLAZE! #17: BAD MEDICINE, Michael Newton

BLAZE! #18: SPANISH GOLD, Benjamin Boulden

*For Kara and Sarah.
The two best girls anywhere*

PROLOGUE

Salt Lake City Trumpeter, March 28, 1875

Itinerant man found mutilated on West Broadway. Playing children discovered the dead body of an adult Indian male in an alley between Bullard's Meat Packing and Carson's Tannery in Salt Lake City late yesterday. Police believe the man's body was dumped in the alley. At current, there are no leads regarding the man's name, or his killers.

Salt Lake City Trumpeter, May 7, 1875

Elder Gareth Davies found dead at his home at 35 E. So. Temple. Elder Davies, born in Cardiff, Wales, England, died May 6 of an accidental fall while repairing the roof of his stable. Elder Davies, member of the Quorum of the Seventy, is best known for his missionary work with the Uinta Valley Ute tribe in Utah's Great Basin. Baptizing more than 50 Ute Indians, he was well-liked for his kindness and humanitarian work when the Ute reservation opened a decade ago. He is survived by his wives, Joanna, Mary, Clara, Alice, and Minnie. He leaves behind a legacy of sixteen children and seven grandchildren. Services to be at the Tabernacle, May 9, 10 a.m.

CHAPTER 1

J.D. Blaze stopped cold at the unusual sound. The night abandoned buildings huddled along the road were made sinister by the moon's eerie glow. The street cast in whispery shadow.

The gunfighter palmed the Colt .44-40 in its cross-draw rig, held his breath to listen. A summer breeze whistled across rough-hewn timber; sweetly scented by sage and juniper. Behind him, disappointed miners shouted when their dice went cold.

J.D. jumped at the miners' voices, his Colt cleared leather in a single smooth motion.

He scowled, shook his head and replaced the big revolver in its holster.

J.D. smiled at the teasing words he imagined Kate would say about his skittishness. When he thought about her, sitting alone in a saloon unfit for anything alive, especially a beautiful woman like Kate, he hustled toward the hotel to complete his task.

But the sound bounced again.

An open-handed slap, fleshy and hard. A wheezing gasp followed by a startled cry and an incomprehensible buzzing whisper.

J.D. bristled, an icy cold awareness crawled up his

spine. A yellow glow at an alley's entrance between a lawyer's shop and mercantile. Shadows wavered across the alley's threshold, long and narrow.

The whispers stopped, then started again before fading into the night's warm breeze. J.D. withdrew the Colt from its holster and walked towards the alley. At its entrance, he stepped from the road to the boardwalk and peeked into the lighted passage.

A man and woman. The woman's back against the wall, her head forward, chin down. The blue gingham dress hitched above her knees to reveal the pale flesh beneath. The man held her chest with his left hand and with the right explored the darker regions below.

The woman strained. Her back arched. Her hips twisted as she tried to escape the man's searching hand. She clasped her fingers together in a fist and punched at her attacker. The blow went wild and skipped harmlessly off his shoulder.

"Goddammit!" the man hissed before crashing a fist into the woman's belly.

Her eyes opened wide with pain, she leaned forward and gagged.

A ghoulish smile crossed the man's face in the light's shadowy flicker. "You're a real gentlelady, ain't you? You ask me, that husband of yours is making a mistake."

The man giggled, tobacco juice dribbled down his chin.

"Please, stop."

J.D. watched the chaos of man and woman for a few moments while he judged the situation.

He moved into the alley, Colt raised and pointed at man's head. "Let the woman go."

The tobacco man jerked at the words. His eyes wide with surprise.

"Who—"

J.D.'s voice rising, "Let her go now!"

The man reached for the iron strapped to his leg. His motion self-conscious and slow.

"You put a finger on that and I'll cut you low!"

Tobacco sputtered. His face blotched red in the alley's syrupy light. Without releasing his grip on the woman, he spun and placed his terrified victim between himself and J.D. The revolver in his hand. Its barrel jabbed the soft flesh beneath the woman's jaw.

"You hold it right there, mister. Any closer and I'll drop her where she stands. A pill in her brain, as certain as a dog'll bark."

The woman stumbled forward.

Tobacco caught her, pulled her against his chest.

"Goddamn bitch!"

J.D. eased his finger from the trigger. He moved to his right for a better angle at the man.

"You hold it. Right now! God. Damnit!" Tobacco, with a herky-jerky wrist motion, swung the gun's barrel from the woman to J.D. and back. His hand shaking so hard J.D. feared an accidental discharge.

J.D. stopped. "No one's going to hurt you. You put the hog leg down and kick it over here, release the woman. If you do that, we all walk away."

Tobacco's eyes bulged. The whites stained yellow with fear, the pupils tiny and hard. His knuckles whitened on the revolver with a tightening grip. Then, surprising J.D., he hollered, "Gentry! Help! Anybody!"

With Tobacco's attention diverted J.D. moved smoothly to his right and opened an angle between the man and his hostage. He aimed the front sight on Tobacco's forehead. He took a breath and pulled the trigger. The Colt bucked in his hand, flames stretched from its barrel. A red splotch appeared in the center of Tobacco's forehead. A gray and red splatter danced on the aging pine boards behind.

The woman fell to her knees, screaming. Her face covered with Tobacco's splattered blood. Panic raged in her eyes as she looked at J.D. and screamed, "They'll kill him!"

She stood on wobbly knees and ran down the alley.

J.D. holstered the Colt. He took three long strides and kicked the revolver from Tobacco's dead hand. He looked up as the woman turned from the alley, but before he could follow a shotgun blast bellowed across the alley. It bounced off the walls and rang in J.D.'s ears.

J.D. froze, one foot slightly in front of the other. He raised his hands above his head.

"On your knees!"

J.D. obeyed.

"Turn around. Nice and slow."

J.D. followed the man's instructions, hands in the air, knees scraping across hardpan, until he was face to face with a wiry-tough man. A shotgun in his hands. Its black bore unblinkingly stared at J.D. A bowler on his head and a bronze star on his chest shimmered the alley's light.

"I'm glad to see you, Sheriff." A good-natured grin on his face.

"I'm sure you are." The man motionless as a snake, his lips hardly moved as he spoke.

A red-faced round man scurried to the lawman's side. "Is he dead?"

"Go check, Randy," the lawman said to the newcomer.

"Sure thing, Sheriff." Randy rushed past J.D. He kneeled next to Tobacco and slapped his face.

J.D. said, "I'm pretty sure he's dead."

"He sure is," Randy said.

"Well," the Sheriff said to J.D., "killing a deputy's a hanging offense in my jurisdiction."

J.D. sighed. His grin disappeared and he cursed under his breath.

CHAPTER 2

The saloon wasn't the sort of place Kate Blaze would choose to sit alone and the longer J.D. was gone the more uncomfortable she became. Unity's male population, which accounted for nine out ten of its inhabitants, worked the silver and gold mines scattered across the plateaued landscape that surrounded the town. The better of the men would be at home on a Wednesday night, readying themselves for another hard day's work. That left the scoundrels, deadbeats and drunkards in a dump like *Petey's Bucket of Blood*.

Kate was thinking all this as she sat at a corner table. Her back against the wall and waited for J.D. to return from his mysterious errand. But she was interrupted by the oddest man she had ever seen. His skin colored alabaster, no hair on his face—not even eyebrows over his pale pink eyes—with a smile as smarmy as any she had seen.

He removed his pristine cap to reveal a smooth and hairless scalp. He bowed at the waist in a practiced motion. "Good evening to you, ma'am."

Kate instinctively pulled her hand away as the man reached across the table for it. She palmed the revolver's cool grip at her waist.

The man's smile widened as he straightened back to his full height, the bowler still in his hand. "I see you are as wary as you are beautiful. Given our surroundings," he gestured to indicate the grubby saloon and its grubbier clientele, "it is wise for such beauty to be wary."

Kate wasn't one to find fault in the appearance of others, but the man's pasty skin, pink eyes and hairless head were unsettling. Even more so was his extreme self-confidence.

"Who are you?" Kate said.

The alabaster colored man performed a pirouette; spinning and straightening in a single poetic motion. "Marcus Guggenheim at your service. Marcus is my given name, but anyone as charming as you should most definitely call me Marc. If it pleases you, that is."

"Marc?"

"Yes, ma'am?"

"Well—"

"May I sit with you?"

Kate removed her hand from the holstered Colt. A suitor, even one as strange as Marcus Guggenheim, she could handle without violence. She smiled and leaned forward in her chair as though she was about to confer a secret. "I appreciate the offer of your company, but my husband is away on a short errand. What I mean is, I would hate for there to be any trouble."

"Trouble? I *am* troubled by the thought of a woman as stunning as you tied to a single man."

His smarmy smile made him look like a fish sucking air.

"My apologies." Kate looked at the saloon's entrance, hoping J.D. would appear. "But I'm not interested."

Guggenheim took the seat next to her, where J.D. had sat only minutes earlier. "I'm sorry, but I seem to have misplaced your name."

Kate laughed. A genuine smile crossed her lips. "You are an odd man. You can't misplace something you've never possessed."

"And you're a wonderful woman." Alabaster leaned closer to Kate, put his hand on her knee and squeezed. An ingratiating smile on his ugly face, pink flames in his eyes betrayed raw desire.

Kate tilted her head girlishly, an affectation she had practiced for years. A breezy mischief in her eyes. She leaned closer to Alabaster and placed her right hand on his inner thigh. Her finger tips danced coyly across his cotton trousers.

Guggenheim gasped. His smile relaxed into a feral grin. He leaned back in the creaky saloon chair, had the audacity to moan.

"You like that?" Kate whispered.

"Shall we—"

Kate found Guggenheim's soft balls and squeezed.

Hard.

Alabaster bucked, tried to stand, but fell back into the chair with a whimper when Kate refused his release. Moaning and squirming, face as purple as a ripened beet, Alabaster balled his left hand and punched at Kate's midsection. Kate moved forward a few inches and Alabaster's knuckles skidded harmlessly off her hip and smashed with a crack against Kate's blackened pine chair.

Alabaster squealed in pain. His face shaded darker. His lips moved silently.

Kate adjusted her grip with a satisfying twist. She leaned forward and whispered plainly into Alabaster's ear, "You ever touch me, talk to me, even look at me again and I'll make sure your little soldiers lose their step." She leaned back, still holding her captives, and glared at Alabaster. "You tracking me, Marc?"

Guggenheim nodded. He gasped between pale lips and

small teeth.

"Did you say something?"

Guggenheim opened his eyes. The pain visible in the chalky pink irises.

"Yeah," he whispered, "I understand."

"Good." Kate released her grip. She good naturedly slapped Guggenheim's cheek. She stood and straightened her clothing while she kept an eye on the still suffering man, patted his bald head.

"I'm glad we have an understanding."

Kate turned and walked to the saloon's exit. The place silent except for the click-clack of her boots on the timbered floor. The jangle of her spurs. Her only thought was the appropriate punishment to be meted out to J.D. for leaving her alone in a cesspool like *Petey's Bucket of Blood*. A few ideas sparkled, but were lost in a pistol shot's echoing rumble.

CHAPTER 3

A group gathered at an alley's entrance and covered the main street's entire width. Kate slowed to a walk as she approached. Her hand firmly on the Colt holstered at her hip. A frenzied excitement filled the air as the men whispered, giggled, pointed and in a few cases, shouted hostilities.

"Kill him!"

"Gut the sumbitch!"

Kate smoothly entered the gathering. She cut a path to the front where she saw J.D. on his knees. His arms stretched high. A nervous look in his eyes as the crowd threatened to become a mob. A fat man paced nervously around a corpse behind J.D. The dead man's blood and brains fresh on the alley's hardpan dirt.

A timber straight man with a professional calm in the night's chaos held a double-barrel scattergun pointed at J.D.

"Kill him, Gentry!"

Gentry, the man with the scattergun, said, "Shut the hell up. All of you! This is my town and any killing will be done in conformity with the law."

Gentry's stillness, his focused concentration on the task, unsettled Kate. He was a professional and that would make him hard to distract. A man uneasily swayed once he had something in his mind. Like J.D. as a murderer. The dead man as a victim.

Kate moved along the mob's face until she stood near the darkened mercantile's front corner. She eased forward a few feet until she caught J.D.'s attention. He looked at her without moving his head. His face expressionless, lips taut.

With his left-hand Gentry retrieved manacles from his belt, held them towards J.D. and the fat man. The shotgun steady and still. Its bead never wavering from J.D.'s chest.

"Okay, Randy. When I tell you, fasten these around his wrists." Gentry tossed the handcuffs underhanded over J.D.'s head. The little man bobbled the handcuffs, dropped them with a clatter to the ground. He glanced at the onlookers with embarrassment, tried his best to ignore a few catcalls—"a chicken leg he'd catch," and "bankers is known for slippery fingers"—and retrieved the irons with obvious self-consciousness.

Gentry said to J.D., "You right handed?"

J.D. nodded.

"I want you to lower your left hand and stretch your arm as far back, behind you, as you can. Keep your right arm high."

"I can do that, Sheriff." J.D. glanced at Kate, shook his head with a nearly imperceptible motion.

Kate understood he was asking her to stand down, to let the scene play out. She moved her hand from the Colt and watched the crowd threaten to burst its seams. She'd seen crowds like this before and it scared her. On a Sunday in Santa Fe when a lookout for a burglary was beaten and hanged by church going folks. Another time in Denver when a little girl was found murdered in a livery stall. The suspect, a slow-witted sixteen-year-old boy, was caught in a copse of trees a few miles from the murder site. Barking dogs treed him like a possum and the townspeople—mothers and fathers, brothers and sisters—pulled him down and tore him to pieces.

J.D. followed Sheriff Gentry's instructions with slow, deliberate movements. His right arm straight in the air, his left stretched behind him, his shoulder dipping. A slight tremor in his arms from the effort.

"Okay, Randy," Sheriff Gentry said when J.D. was in the requested position. "Walk up on him slow and place the iron on his wrist. Make sure you lock it."

Randy's nervous tension was obvious. His hands shook. His breath whistled from his mouth. His eyes wide, pupils bounced. A few feet shy of J.D., Randy stopped and reached for J.D.'s wrist. It took a moment, but finally the handcuff clacked closed. Randy turned the key.

"Okay. It's locked," Randy said.

The crowd watched the procedure. Its anxious demeanor calmed by the activity.

"Now, mister. I want you to. And damn slowly," Sheriff Gentry said to J.D. "Reach back with your other hand so Randy can finish the job."

"Yes, sir." J.D. lowered his right arm. He put it behind his back.

Randy, steadier now that J.D. hadn't made a fuss, snapped the right cuff closed and locked it with a single quick movement. The little man wiped sweat from his brow with the sleeve of his fancy boiled shirt. A smile tremored his face. He whispered something, to himself or J.D., Kate couldn't tell, and took a step back.

The Sheriff lowered his shotgun. He glared at J.D. for a long moment before he turned his attention to the crowd. His eyes stopped on Kate for a beat before moving on.

"There's nothing to see here. I want every last one of you back where you came from."

The crowd grumbled and whispered disappointment at the missed violence.

"He killed Deputy Haskins." The voice from a lean man in fancy black duds, red vest beneath his dark waistcoat. A riverboat gambler's hat at an angle on his head. "We can't let that sit."

Sheriff Gentry adjusted the belt at his waist, where, Kate noticed, he carried no firearm. "He'll be dealt with, but not here. Not on the street. He'll be taken to the jail and when the judge arrives there'll be a trial. And only then, after he's found guilty will he hang."

The gambler scowled. His hand on the fancy silver-plated Colt worn low on his hip, tied-down like a gunfighter.

"That goes for you, too, Timmons!" The lawman pointed the scattergun at the outspoken dude. "You best mind your manners and go back to the *Wanderlust*."

A vein thundered in the gambler's temple. He studied Gentry for several seconds. Then visibly settled himself. He removed his hand from his fancy gun. "A better idea I've not heard all night, Sheriff. I'm sure you'll satisfactorily take care of this"—his eyes darted to the dead man—"shameful criminal act."

Gentry turned back to J.D. He dismissed Timmons and the crowd as if everyone had faded away. "Can you stand? Or does Randy need to help you?"

"I can stand." It was awkward, and took J.D. a few seconds, but he gained his feet. His arms twisted behind his back. Wrists manacled like a criminal.

The Sheriff took J.D.'s elbow with his left hand, the shotgun firmly in the right, and led him from the alley.

As the small procession passed Kate, J.D. smiled briefly,

whispered, "Get me out."

Kate nodded. She watched as the crowd dispersed back to the saloons, gambling and cat houses. Smiles on their faces. The stories beginning in earnest. They all wondered when the hanging would be. They felt alive at the violence. Everyone in motion, moving towards something. Away from a mob and back to their individual vices.

As Kate turned toward the hotel, she noticed Guggenheim's solitary, motionless figure. Alabaster. As he leaned against a hitching post, a cold, humorless smile on his lips. Her hand instinctively moved back to her Colt. Her palms uncharacteristically damp.

"Mrs. Blaze?"

Kate jumped at the voice. She turned to see a boy. Maybe fifteen. His skin dark, black hair cut short. A red bandanna tied across his brow.

"Kate Blaze?"

Kate looked back to where Alabaster stood moments before, but the street and boardwalk were empty. Night abandoned buildings. Men's backs as they walked slowly in the other direction, none were Guggenheim. His disappearance unnerved Kate more than his presence had.

Kate turned back to the boy. She worked up a smile. "Yes?"

"You're Kate Blaze?"

"That's me. Who are you?"

"I knew it was you and J.D. when I saw you ride into town." His smile burst large. "I'm Joshua." The boy stepped forward and offered his hand in greeting.

Kate cocked her head, her smile widened with sincerity. She wiped her hand on her trouser leg and grasped the boy's. "You don't look like a Joshua to me."

The boy found an interest in the scuffed moccasins on

his feet. His embarrassment's warm haze palpable to Kate.

"I guess you'd know your name better than anybody else."

Joshua's smile brightened. The excitement clear in his voice. "I've read all about you, Mrs. Blaze. And J.D., too."

"Oh yeah?" Kate knew what J.D. would say at that moment, his voice clear in her head—"Don't believe anything you read, kid."—but she had a higher opinion of the written word. "A few of those stories are a bit exaggerated, I'm afraid."

Joshua nodded. His smile a permanent fixture. "I know what happened, Mrs. Blaze. I saw everything."

"Please call me Kate, Joshua. You mean you saw what happened to that man?" Kate pointed to the dead man. The portly banker looked uncomfortable standing over the body.

"Yes, ma'am. I mean, Mrs. Kate. I saw what happened."

CHAPTER 4

The smell of gun oil, sweat and shit permeated J.D.'s cell. He wrinkled his nose and looked around the small rectangular room. An iron bed along one wall, a distressed straw-mattress across its top and a half-full piss bucket were the cell's only furnishings. J.D. sat on the bed, the mattress ineffectively padding its hard iron skeleton. He rubbed his forehead with a dirty hand.

"Well," J.D. said to no one. "I guess this is home for now."

"Not too long is my bet."

A man J.D. hadn't seen when he entered the jail stood on the locked door's other side. He was big with a heavy gut. A smile on his weathered face and a badge pinned to a worn leather vest.

"The judge's regular route puts him in town on Friday." The man's smile spread to his eyes. "I reckon it'll make for a Saturday hanging. Picnics, parties. An affair for the whole family."

J.D. grunted.

"What's that?" The man leaned in, his big mouth between two bars. "You say something?"

J.D. looked at the man, saw the cruel set of his eyes. His red and blue veined nose. "I didn't say anything. Must be my dinner settling. You ever eat at *Petey's*? I can't say much for the atmosphere. The place is a dump, but they serve a good steak."

"A real wise guy, huh?" The man reached for a large key ring on his belt. He thumbed through the keys before finding the right one. He shoved it in the lock, turned it until the latch clacked open.

J.D. sat causally on the bed, watching. "You have a name?"

The big man paused. The key still in the lock. "My name?"

"Now that I think about it, I never introduced myself, either." J.D. stood up from the bed. His head nearly touched the cell's ceiling. "My name's Blaze. J.D. Blaze."

The man fumbled with the key in the lock, his gaze never left J.D. "What did you say your name is?"

J.D. gave a harmless, aw-shucks smile. "J.D. Blaze."

The man smiled like a dummy. An incisor on his lower jaw looked rotten. A dull gleam in his eyes. "I'll be. J.D. Blaze. You're famous, ain't you?"

J.D. grinned. "Yeah, a little."

"I heard about that gunfight you had down in Small Basin."

"Which one?"

A mean look crossed the man's face. "I heard you killed that old sumbitch Skousen."

"That was my wife."

"She with you?"

J.D. looked around the cell. "Not that I can see."

"A real smart ass. I've heard that about you."

"I like to think I'm less smart ass and more misunderstood."

"Come Saturday, we'll see how smart you are."

"You the jailer here?"

The man nodded. He scratched his belly and frowned. The expression made him look like a colicky baby after a long night.

"They give you a badge for that?" J.D. moved his feet wider, preparing. "Or is that tin on your chest borrowed from your daughter's play things?"

It took a moment. J.D. counted to six, in fact, but the words finally burrowed their way into the man's skull. He tilted his head. A red flame rose in his eyes.

"You son of—"

He didn't finish the thought, instead the man swung the door open. He ducked his head through the doorway and lumbered into the cell. His hands outstretched and aiming for J.D.'s neck. J.D. ducked to his left and caught the man with a sharp right to the belly. The jailer gasped, spittle flew from his gaping mouth. His hands clutched at his belly as he fell backwards. J.D. kicked him in the shoulder. The jailer slammed against the wall where he slid to the floor. His eyes still open. His rage replaced with bright pain.

J.D. moved past the jailer and into the outer room. A kerosene lamp licked light across the plank floor. J.D. turned left. The doorway into the office straight ahead.

"Frank?"

J.D. stopped.

His hand instinctively went to where the Colt would normally be strapped on his left side. He found only empty belt. He glanced back at the fallen jailer. No gun in sight. He looked around the room for a weapon and settled on a broom leaning against the back wall. When it was in his hands, the handle broke with a crack across his right knee.

J.D. held the broomstick like a bat and moved cautiously toward the brightly lit doorway.

He paused, listened. The place quiet as a grave. No voices, no creaking floor boards. Nothing except the jailer's soft mewling. J.D. stared at the doorway. Its inviting glow urged him forward. He knew it was a trap. One man, maybe more, waited for him on the other side, but it was his only way out.

J.D. took a hesitant step. He flinched as a board cracked under his foot, but kept walking. He stayed on his toes until he stood a few feet from the door.

Stopped, listened.

Silence. Brooding and false in J.D.'s ears.

He took a deep breath and ducked low towards the doorway's left side and crossed the threshold.

CHAPTER 5

Kate said, "Tell me what you saw."

Joshua squirmed with pleasure under Kate's gaze. A smile plastered on his face.

"Please tell me Joshua." Kate grasped the boy's shoulder in her hand. She lowered her voice to a whisper, forced a calmness into it she didn't feel. "J.D.'s life may depend on it."

The boy told Kate everything he'd seen. J.D.'s discovery of the man and woman in the alleyway. The shooting and the woman's flight.

"You know the rest." The boy gained confidence with each word he spoke.

Kate ruffled his hair. "Have you ever seen the woman before tonight?"

Joshua nodded.

Kate stopped herself from chuckling at the boy's reticence and seeming desire to have her pry every piece of information from him. "Who is she?"

"She's new in town." His voice high, excited.

"Is she alone, Joshua? Or is she here with someone?"

Joshua shook his head. "She has a husband, but he's out there."

Kate waited for more, but when it became apparent the

boy was finished she said, "Joshua, where's 'out there'?"

"Oh." Joshua nodded his head so hard Kate thought his nose was going to come loose. "The white fathers sold him land near the reservation. He is there now. He wants to be a farmer, I think."

"What's her name?"

Joshua shook his head.

Kate said, "Do you know where she lives?"

He looked at his moccasins, kicked at the dirt. "I'm sorry."

Kate smiled. She squeezed his shoulder again and lifted his face up until his eyes met hers. "Don't be sorry. You've been a great help."

Kate glanced at the man called Randy standing over the corpse in the alley, then back to the boy. "I need some help. Do you think you can help me?"

His smile returned, white teeth shimmered in the moonlight. "Yes, ma'am."

"Wait for me while I go talk to the that man." Kate motioned toward Randy with her thumb.

Joshua said, "Mr. Christensen?"

"The Sheriff called him Randy. Is that his name?"

The boy nodded, Kate smiled.

"Wait here." With a relaxed gait Kate started towards the pacing man. An approachable, innocent cast to her eyes. A softness around her mouth. It has her virginal look, and Kate knew men enjoyed it nearly as much as her raffish, man-eating persona.

Randy Christensen watched Kate approach. A startled glint in his eyes. He opened his mouth as if to speak, but closed it without words. The night's silence so deep Kate heard the wet sound his tongue made as it settled in his mouth. He looked from Kate's eyes to the Colt strapped on her hip and back. Tension obvious in his darting, unsteady gaze.

"Mr. Christensen?"

"Ah—" His voice sour with fear.

"Randy?"

Finally, he said, "Yes, ma'am. That's me. Randy."

Kate stopped a few feet short. She dropped her most seductive smile and twirled her blonde ponytail with her left hand. "I bet you are."

Randy gulped, wheezed. His eyes nearly boggled from his head. "Pardon?"

"What happened here tonight?" Kate pointed at the prostrate corpse. "To him, I mean?"

"Well. You see. He was…umm. Shot, I mean."

"By you?" Kate tilted her head as if she was reevaluating the man's potential. His potency.

He stood a little straighter, Kate noticed, and spoke a little clearer. "No, ma'am. Another fellow shot him. I'm just watching him for the Sheriff."

"What could happen? He's already dead, isn't he?" Kate stepped closer to the portly man. "My name's Kate."

Randy's eyes went wide with something between fear and pleasure. "Kate?"

"Yes?"

"Yes?" Confusion in Randy's eyes now.

"I thought you were asking a question." Kate reached across. She placed her fingertips on his round cheek.

Randy stammered. He stepped back half a pace and brought his hand up to where Kate's fingers had been. He rubbed at it a few times.

"No— No questions."

"So, what happened?"

"Well, you see. There was a shooting."

"Do you know who this man is?" Kate's voice lowering in volume with each word.

Randy leaned in closer to hear better. "Yes, ma'am. Kate. This is. Was, Deputy Billy Haskins."

Kate's eyebrows raised, an "o" formed on her lips. "You must be trustworthy for the Sheriff to leave a deputy in your care?"

A sliver of smile crossed Randy's face. "Nothing special. Just helping out where I can."

"Are you a deputy, too?"

Randy tugged at his trousers. He hitched them up a few inches. "Not me. Nothing more than a bank clerk."

"I'm sure." Kate put a hand on his arm.

Randy noticed, looking at Kate's hand with both fear and delight.

"I heard there was a woman here, too. When the shooting happened, I mean. Is that true?"

Randy, his eyes never leaving Kate's hand on his arm, said, "Well, there was someone running down the alley when me and Sheriff Gentry come around the corner."

Kate removed her hand from Randy's arm. She wanted him looking at her eyes, and he did. "You know who it was?"

"No, ma'am." An odd look clouded Randy's face. His forehead scrunched up as if he were thinking. "Why are you asking?"

"I'm a terrible gossip." Kate giggled. A mischievous smile touched her red lips. "I'm sorry. My mother taught me better, but her lessons never took, I guess."

Randy's eyes twinkled. He laughed nervously and belched. His face turned tomato red. "Sorry, I guess my dinner and all the excitement got the better of me."

Kate laughed. She liked this odd, shy little man.

"Nothing to be sorry about. I need your help."

Randy looked at the dead deputy at his feet. "I can't really leave until…"

"It's nothing that will require you to abandon your duty."

Randy nodded enthusiastically.

Kate continued, "You see, I'm new in town. Arrived just today. I came to see a friend, but somewhere between Denver and here I misplaced her address. Do you think you could help?"

Randy nodded. His gaze on Kate's mouth. "I can sure try."

"Oh, thank you, Randy. I'm so relieved I found such a charming fellow."

Randy smiled, a smitten cast at its upturned edges.

"My friend came with her husband a few months ago. He—I suppose I should say 'they' in this enlightened age—purchased farm land out near the reservation."

Randy's smile grew so large, Kate could see his tonsils bounce. "Why, I surely do know your friends. Stephen Wiley. He opened an account at the bank so I know him. You're friends with his Emma?"

"That's them!" Kate looked at the ground, then back at Randy with tentative shyness. "I'm such a forgetful person I swear I'd lose my own head if it wasn't attached. If I don't find their place before long I won't have anywhere to stay the night."

Randy beamed. Joy in his voice as he regained position in the conversation. "Between you and me, I'm the same way. Emma's living in Mrs. Teller's house. It's technically a house for single women, but since Stephen left for the Basin—that's where his, err…*their* land is located—Emma may as well be single."

Kate thanked the portly banker for his kindness and

turned back into the street where Joshua waited in the shadows on the other side. Her eyes scanned the street's silver-lighted horizon for any threats, for the alabaster man. There was nothing except Joshua's white teeth reflecting moonlight. An obvious smile on his shadow-darkened face, and Kate could only smile back even as her thoughts turned hard at what needed to be done to get J.D. out of the noose sliding around his neck.

CHAPTER 6

J.D. crashed through the doorway. He skidded a few feet on his bootheels and smashed into a wooden chair and knocked it over with a clatter. The broom handle firmly in his right hand, perpendicular with the floor. The small rectangular room empty except for two battle worn desks and four uncomfortable looking wooden chairs blackened with age. The outside door straight ahead. Its glass front beckoned him into the open night.

J.D. forced himself to slow down. Often a dire situation could be avoided with a little thought. He looked around the room and noticed his Colt. It was wrapped in its gun belt and sat atop the nearest pock-marked desk. A smile found J.D.'s mouth; he whispered, "You've got to be kidding me."

"No jokes. It's yours if you can get to it."

J.D. jerked with surprise. He looked at the Colt a few feet away and then over his shoulder to where the voice had come from. Sheriff Gentry stepped from a narrow crevice between the wall and a cabinet. The same two-shot gun from the alley in his hands. Its large black barrels stared at J.D. like angry eyes.

"Well?"

J.D. sighed. He raised his hands above his head. "You got me again, Sheriff."

"I sure do, Mr. Blaze. Now, I need you to stand very still and keep your arms straight in the air."

J.D. followed orders—something he was growing uncomfortably accustomed to—and planted a grin on his face more out habit than anything else. "I shouldn't be surprised at the sound of my name since that—" He paused to search for a fancy Kate-approved word, "Neanderthal. The big fellow in the back room, had me figured in three minutes."

The Sheriff pulled manacles from a hook on the wall to his right. He tossed them to J.D.

"Put those on."

J.D. said, "I'll have to move."

"This scattergun tells me you'll be nice and slow about it."

J.D. picked the heavy wrist manacles off the floor. He clamped the left handcuff closed.

"I need to hear it click."

J.D. snapped it closed with a loud clack. "You're a careful bastard."

"My mother's affairs are none of your concern, Mr. Blaze."

"Call me J.D."

"I'll leave it as *Mr. Blaze* for now. It's difficult to be cordial with the man who killed my deputy." Gentry motioned towards the wall with his scattergun. "Now, step over there. Keep your arms stretched high."

J.D. turned to his left and took two short steps to the interior wall. The lawman on his right, a scratchy blur in his peripheral vision.

"Now what?"

"I want your hands as high on that wall as you can reach."

A splinter from the wall's decorative wood paneling pierced J.D.'s right palm as he obliged.

"Spread your legs and lean forward until your forehead's against the wall."

J.D. was off-balance without any hope of making a play for the lawman. Gentry's blurred form disappeared from J.D.'s peripheral vision. The clack of bootheels on wood echoed behind him. J.D. tensed as he anticipated a painful blow to a kidney, maybe his head.

Gentry's voice a soft whisper behind J.D., two feet away at the most. "Bring your left hand behind your back."

J.D. hesitated a moment.

"I wouldn't." The lawman's voice louder than before. "I have no compunction about splattering your blood on these walls."

J.D. pulled his left hand away from the wall and brought it down in a slow arc until his knuckles touched his lower back.

"Good."

The room went silent. J.D.'s breathing heavy in his own ears.

The clatter of steel on wood. A stabbing pain as Gentry dug a knee into J.D.'s back and smashed him tight against the wall. His left wrist jerked painfully up. His right hand yanked from the wall with enough force to make J.D. curse. Before the expletive was born he felt the iron manacle clack closed with white hot pain across both wrists.

Gentry released and stepped away from J.D in a single smooth motion.

J.D. stumbled. He tried to bring his arms up to catch his balance, but the iron handcuffs held them tight at his back with crystal pain. He took two short steps to his left, faded backwards and struck a chair below his right knee. He fell on his back with a heavy thud.

The impact brought stars to J.D.'s vision. Electric pain arced in his wrists and arms.

After what seemed like several minutes J.D. opened his eyes. His vision blurred, the cold white pinpricks receded to its edges. The shadowy ceiling beams came into focus, then Sheriff Gentry's bare head came into view. A grim smile on his face.

"We need to talk."

"I can talk." J.D.'s voice seemed to quaver in his own ears. "Do I get to sit on a chair? Or am I supposed to lay on the floor all night?"

Gentry helped J.D. stand. He righted the chair that had caused the excitement and pointed to it.

"Sit."

J.D. sat. The chair's backrest to his right. His hands dangled behind him in the air.

Gentry, his steely eyes never wavering from J.D., opened the desk's center drawer. He pulled a small tin of cigarette makings out, built a smoke, torched it with a lucifer and took a pull. His chair squeaked when he leaned back.

"Frank?" Gentry's eyes remained on J.D.

A groan in response.

"You okay?"

"Son of a bitch."

"I think he's questioning your mother's integrity." A twinkle in Gentry's eyes caught J.D. off guard. "I guess you get what you throw."

J.D. nodded. "Sounds like it, but I won't tell my mom if you don't."

"That's a promise." Gentry leaned forward and placed both elbows on his desk. "What happened out there?"

J.D. sat silently. The only movement his still labored

breathing. He stared at the lawman while trying to hide his surprise at the question.

Gentry said, "I'm new here. I inherited Billy. The deputy you killed. I didn't trust him much, and I know about you, Mr. Blaze. You're a hard man and a killer, but you generally end up on the right side. So, I'm asking you, why'd you kill Billy?"

"I may need a lawyer before I get all cuddly with you, Sheriff. No offense, but this isn't my first interrogation."

"None taken." Gentry took another drag on his smoke, held it near the desktop and watched its bright orange tip fade. "Not a lawyer in the whole town, Mr. Blaze."

"No lawyers? I could settle in a town like that."

"I can't say I'd recommend it. I've been here six weeks and have yet to find a solitary thing to like about the place." He flicked cigarette ash on the floor.

"Not even *Petey's*?"

Gentry smiled to reveal white teeth. "I guess I overlooked *Petey's*. A shithole, if I've ever seen one, but they do fry a nice steak."

"Mine was still moving when they served it."

Gentry leaned back in his chair, brushed something unseen from his lap. "We don't have much time, Mr. Blaze. Maybe twenty-four hours until the circuit judge makes his appearance, say another twelve before you're swinging at the end of a rope. And I wouldn't like to see that. Not at all. I think we can help each other."

The Sheriff brought the homemade to his mouth, took a pull. "There's something not right around here. The town's sour. And I think you can help me find out what's behind it."

A nice speech, thought J.D., from a man who, if he was any judge of character, spoke sparingly at best.

From the back room Frank the jailer coughed. A clock on the wall click-clacked away the seconds. The darkness outside the office windows seemed to thicken, close itself around J.D. and the lawman.

J.D. said, "These manacles are chafing. Any chance you can take them—"

J.D. heard the big man a fraction before he felt bare knuckles crash against his jaw. The chair rocked, its front leg shattered. J.D. hit the floor. Pain blistered in his shoulder, arced down his spine and blossomed across his right hip. His head smashed against Gentry's desk, bounced. Stars sizzled across his vision, faded to gray, then black.

CHAPTER 7

The large Victorian clapboard appeared dilapidated in the moon's glow. Rotting pine boards peeked out from beneath peeling paint. The roof's shaking cracked and curled. Despair scuttled in Kate's chest as she stepped onto the long porch. The boards whimpered with each step. Kate paused at the door to listen, but heard nothing other than her own breathing and the gentle whispering breeze.

Kate knocked on the door softly. She waited several seconds without response and rapped again.

The hushed sound of footfalls on protesting floorboards.

"Who is it?" The words shallow across the door's barrier.

"Kate Blaze. I'm here to see Emma Wiley, ma'am."

A latch clicked, the doorknob turned hesitantly. A streak of calm light filled a widening gap between door and jamb as the door opened inward. The woman cast a shadow across the narrow opening.

"It's quite late." A pleasing Irish lilt.

"I know, ma'am. And I'm sorry about that, but it's very important I speak with Mrs. Wiley."

Kate stepped away from the door, hoping the move would ease any doubt the woman had.

"Are you Mrs. Teller?"

The woman nodded, opened the door a few more inches.

"You're alone?"

"Yes— Well, no. There's a boy with me, but he's waiting back on the road."

The door began to close.

"Randy Christensen told me I would find Emma here, Mrs. Teller."

The woman hesitated a moment, then pulled the door inward revealing her narrow frame covered with a threadbare pink cotton nightdress.

"Randy? He sent you here?"

"Randy said Emma lived here in your home."

"This hasn't been a home since my dear Jonathon passed from this world six long years ago." Her mouth pinched unpleasantly.

Laudanum's bitter smell on the woman's voice.

"I'm sorry about your loss."

"Yes, I suppose you are. Emma is upstairs in her room. She came home late tonight for reasons unknown to me." Mrs. Teller's eyes faded away from Kate as she spoke. "A friend of Randy's is welcome here, even at such a late hour."

Kate held the urge to check her clasp watch, knowing the hour was somewhere past ten.

"Please come in. Your name is Kate?"

"Yes, Mrs. Teller. I'm Kate Blaze."

"I'll fetch dear Emma."

Mrs. Teller walked up narrow stairs, seeming to float in her long nightdress, her feet hidden beneath its worn material.

Kate stood in the dim entryway, a small oil lamp ineffectually flickered at shadows from the next room. A heartsick weariness settled on her as thoughts of J.D. sitting in a jail cell intruded. A judge and then a rope in his future.

Footsteps on the landing above pulled Kate's attention back to the moment. A whispering, unintelligible conversation. A guttural scream. What sounded like an open-handed slap.

"Is everything okay, Mrs. Teller?"

Kate stepped towards the stairs. She palmed the Colt with practiced efficiency.

"No!" The word echoed off the walls.

Kate scrambled up the steps, two at a time. Her boots pounded on bare wood runners. Above, an angry scraping as a window opened.

"Please, Emma. Please don't." Mrs. Teller's voice shrill with fear.

A heavy thump, followed by rattling glass. A gentle vibration in the floor beneath Kate's feet. She paused, uncertain if she should continue upwards to the second floor or go down and outside.

"She go out the window?" Kate hollered.

The entire house shook, windows rattled, dust and dirt jumped, as hurried footsteps pounded across the roof. Kate turned back down the stairs. She jumped the several feet to the entryway floor. Her knees absorbed the hard landing. She steadied herself, then slammed through the door and into the moonlit night.

Across the street Jacob stood with wide-spread legs, pointing to Kate's left.

"Over there!"

Kate ran along the front porch. The Colt still tight in her hand. Ahead she heard a grunt followed by a cracking tree limb and a cry.

"Oh please. Ohpleaseohplease." The words running together in fear and pain.

Kate reached the porch's edge and jumped. The .44's front sight tracking Emma's wreathing form.

Kate hit the ground.

She fell to her knees before toppling onto her backside. The Colt never wavered from its target.

"Hold it, Emma! Don't you even think about moving."

Kate rose to a knee and then found her feet. Raw pain prickled her palm, blossomed up her arm. The Colt steady, she eased towards the fallen girl.

"Are you okay?"

The girl, flat on her back, arms around her right knee, looked up. A silvery tear luminescent in the moon's glow.

"Emma—"

A booming roar shattered the night. Kate dropped hard to the ground on hands and knees, pain grappled at her head from the blast. A howling buzz in her ears. The Colt skittered from her grasp.

Kate pulled up short when cold steel touched the back of her neck.

"Hold it right there." The words shouted, but in Kate's overwhelmed senses they were soft, muddled.

Kate sat back on her haunches. She raised her hands above her head.

"One move and I'll kill you. I really will, Kate Blaze."

CHAPTER 8

Clomping feet, buzzing whispers. A metallic clicking as someone played with a gun's hammer.

"Would you s-stop that?" A stammering voice said.

"I'm nervous is all."

"Yeah? Well, you're making me nervous, too. S-so put that away before somebody gets hurt."

A grunt. Steel on leather. "Satisfied?"

"Jes-sus."

J.D.'s confusion built rapidly and rushed toward panic. He opened an eye. The world fuzzy, twisting into the absurd. He slowed his breathing, closed his eye again. He thought about Kate on her own in a strange and dangerous town. She could handle herself, always had, but still he worried and hoped she was okay and had a plan to get him out.

He opened his eye again. A slit this time. Above he saw the ceiling's unfinished wood. Cell bars surrounding him. The bed's iron end posts. His head throbbed, scorching pain flared in his jaw with every heartbeat. He kept still, silent.

A door squeaked open, closed.

A different voice. "That's Blaze in the back?"

"Yep." The voice belonged to Nervous, J.D thought.

Heavy footsteps approached. Stopped. J.D. heard a rattle. The snick of a key sliding into the locking mechanism.

"Gentry won't like it if you open that door," Stammer said.

"Gentry ain't here, is he?"

The key turned. The tumblers rolled, the lock clacked open. J.D. took a deep breath. He tensed the muscles in his arms and legs and rolled his neck slightly. The motion caused the pounding in his head to flare. Nausea threatened to overwhelm him. His head spun. He closed his eyes again, breathed.

The door started to open on squeaking hinges.

"I'm telling you, Gentry won't like what you're doing." Stammer's voice high-pitched with tension.

"Shit, Harry. You sound like an old woman. Don't he, Frank?"

"Blaze is a tough son of a bitch." J.D. connected Nervous as Frank the jailer.

"He sure looks tough. What'd you hit him with, Frank? An anvil?"

Frank giggled.

The stranger stepped into the cell, floorboards whimpered under his weight.

Frank said, "I sure got him good. I sure did."

"You want another shot at him?"

"Yeah. Yeah." The words dripped with anticipation.

"There he is. Just waiting for—"

The outer door swung open. Bootheels on wood echoed across the office, slow at first and then hurried.

"The hell you two think you're doing?" Sheriff Gentry burst through the door between the office and jail, grabbed Frank by his collar and yanked him backwards.

Frank gasped, stumbled against the wall.

J.D., eyes open now, started to get up. His vision went dark at the edges. He fell back on the bed. Pain rushed across his back and shoulders. His head pounded. The smell of shit and piss nauseating in the small cell. He leaned over the bed and vomited.

"Shit!" the stranger said.

"You close that damn door, Sully."

"Did you see that, Sheriff? The big hero spilled his guts all over the floor."

J.D., on his hands and knees, watched as the Sheriff stepped closer to Sully. He pulled a slim double-sided knife from his belt. "Close the door. Right. Now."

Sully's eyes narrowed. His right hand dropped to the hog leg strapped low on his hip. He looked from Gentry to the blade and back. A wildness in his eyes.

"Shit. I was only kidding around, Gentry." The decision made. He moved his hand away from his gun. "You're always so damn serious."

"Get out!" Gentry moved back a step. "Right now. If I see you in this office again I'll carve you like a pig."

Sully stood still. His face burning anger at the insult. A vein throbbed in his temple. His hand wavered above his six-shooter as he weighed his chances against the lawman a second time in as many seconds.

"Pull it." Gentry's voice mild, soft. "Pull it, Sully. Let's see how fast you really are."

Sully's left eye twitched. He took a shuddering breath and pulled his hand away from his iron. "Just having some fun is all."

Gentry motioned to the door into the office. "Outside. Now."

Sully walked from the jail and through the office; one

hand on the door and the other on his six-gun. He turned back to Gentry.

"You're done here, Sheriff. D-O-N-E. You're going to be laid out in the undertaker's window before the week's out just like that piece of shit Jones."

"I'm glad you can spell, Sully." A shotgun appeared in the lawman's hands, both barrels looked at Sully.

"What do you know about Jones?"

With a petulant smile, Sully said, "I know he was tougher and smarter than you'll ever be, Sheriff."

"You kill him?" Gentry's eyes hard.

"You'll never know, Gentry. At least not while you're breathing."

Gentry's face rigid. His finger on the scatter's rear trigger. He breathed, removed his finger from the trigger without lowering the gun. "Get to hell out of my office."

Sully stood in the doorway, straddling the threshold. J.D. leaned against the cell's doorframe. He saw the hatred and fear in Sully's eyes. He knew men like this were trouble. Proud and fearful. They hated the world for their shortcomings. The type that waited for the right moment, came at a man's back from a blind alley without warning to plow slugs into his back.

Sheriff Gentry took a step towards Sully. He raised the shotgun to his shoulder, pulled the hammer back with a click. "Get!"

Sully made a shallow salute and ducked out the door. "I'll being seeing you, Sheriff."

J.D. said, "I don't think he likes you, Gentry."

"Shut up, Blaze." Gentry leaned his shotgun against the wall and stepped quickly to where Frank stood. He slapped the big man hard across the face, put a knee in his nuts.

Frank dropped like a rag doll. He squirmed into the fetal

position and gasped for breath.

"You chicken shit asshole. I'm done with you. Get your fat ass off my floor and get out. You're fired."

Frank, holding his testes, face a ripened tomato, opened his mouth to speak, but whimpered instead.

Gentry turned away and retrieved the shotgun from the wall and marched back to his desk.

The other lawman, Stammer, at the other desk, watched with keen interest. A shadowy smile on his face.

"S-Sheriff?" Stammer said quietly.

Gentry nearly shouted. "What is it, Harry?"

"The cell's still open."

"That's so Frank can clean it out before he leaves." He sat heavily in his chair. "You hear that, Frank? Before you leave, clean that goddamn cell up."

Frank grunted.

"You may as well come out and have a seat, Blaze."

"You trust me?"

"No, but I still have my two-shoot and I'm pretty good with it."

CHAPTER 9

Kate still as a statue. Her hands steady in the air above her head. The hair on her neck and arms standing straight, cold fear icing her eyes. Emma's pain filled cries burned Kate's ears. She felt more than heard the shooter step away, imagined the crunch of gravel, a gun's hammer locking back.

"Mrs. Teller?"

"Hush up, young lady. My Jonathon taught me to shoot and I have one more barrel." Then to Emma, still squirming on the ground, her right knee pulled tight against her chest, "Are you hurt, dear?"

Emma looked up at Mrs. Teller. "It's my knee. It hurts bad."

"I told you not to go out that window."

"Yes, ma'am." Her voice heavy with tears and pain.

"Can you stand?"

Emma rolled onto her hands and knees. She gasped with pain when her right knee touched dirt.

"I can help you, Em—"

"You be still, now." Mrs. Teller's words harsh and angry. The shotgun steady against her shoulder. Its cold eyes never wavered from Kate's center.

"I'm not here to hurt either of you, Mrs. Teller." Then

Kate said to Emma, "The man in the alley. The one that stopped Deputy Haskins from raping you? His name's J.D. and he's my husband. The Sheriff arrested him for murdering the deputy and if you don't tell them what happened they'll hang him."

Emma groaned. She planted her right palm against the house for support.

"I can't have that, Emma. J.D.'s a good man. I need you to tell Sheriff Gentry what happened."

Emma sobbed with fear and turmoil. Her body shook.

"Is this true, Emma?" Mrs. Teller's voice stronger with each word. "Deputy Haskins— Did he..."

"He—" Emma's words broke into a guttural wail.

Kate's heart broke for Emma. The young woman on hands and knees. Her body racked with sobs.

Kate turned to the landlady. "Let me help her into the house, Mrs. Teller."

The older woman sighed and lowered the scattergun. Her body sagged. "I nearly killed you."

Kate pushed herself up. "No one's hurt past recovery. Not from anything." The last words were spoken to Emma.

Kate moved to where her Colt lay in the dirt. Its barrel glowed in the moonlight. When she bent down to retrieve it, Mrs. Teller tensed and raised the shotgun back to her shoulder and then lowered it.

"I'm sorry." Mrs. Teller stepped to the house and leaned the scattergun against the wall. She rubbed her palms across her dress.

Kate retrieved the Colt. She studied it for a moment and when she was satisfied its barrel was free from obstructions she slid it into leather. She scanned the area for any observers, any threats. She saw only the night shrouded expanse of the home's acreage and Joshua moving from one foot to the other at the property's edge. She waved to the boy and called him over.

"Who's the boy?" Mrs. Teller said as Joshua scampered toward the house.

He stopped ten feet from the group and looked inquiringly at Kate.

"This is Joshua. He's been very helpful to me tonight."

The boy studied his moccasins for a moment.

Kate motioned to the two women. "Joshua, this is Mrs. Teller and Emma Wiley. Is Emma the woman you saw earlier tonight with Deputy Haskins?"

"Yes, Mrs. Kate. That's the woman I saw in the alley."

Kate turned to the fallen girl. "Emma?"

Emma sat in the dirt with her back to the wall. She wiped her face with the long sleeve of her modest gingham dress. Kate kneeled next to Emma and wiped a tear from the girl's cheek.

"It's okay. Everything's fine. I promise."

Kate found a frilly white handkerchief in a shirt pocket. A gift from J.D. She studied it before handing it to Emma. The girl pushed it against her face to cover her eyes and mouth.

"Did he hurt you?" Mrs. Teller's voice only a few feet behind Kate, soft and kind.

Emma nodded, but said, "No."

Mrs. Teller turned to Joshua. "Did that scoundrel Haskins hurt her?"

The boy seemed to shrink into himself without moving at all.

Kate, looking over her shoulder at Mrs. Teller, said, "We can talk inside. Help me get her in the house." Then to Emma, "It will be more comfortable for all us."

A smile flittered across Emma's lips.

Kate stood and held her hand down to Emma. "Take my hand."

Mrs. Teller moved next to Emma and took the girl's left elbow in her hands. "When Kate has you up, put your arm around my shoulder and we'll walk into the house together."

The girl nodded. Her face silver in the moonlight.

CHAPTER 10

The Sheriff's Office sat on Main Street. A squat brick building deeper than it was wide. A diner on one side, an assay office on the other. Its windows glowed bright with lamplight on the otherwise dark street. Kate, buried in shadow, studied the office from across the way. A rangy man stepped from its door. He looked up and down the street before he casually leaned against a post at the boardwalk's edge. He pulled a small tin box from his shirt pocket and built a smoke. He lit it and tossed the spent lucifer to the street.

After a few pulls he pushed his hat back on his head and began pacing; five steps down, five steps back. He did this over and over. The homemade never leaving his lips, smoke trailing away in widening blue curls. His eyes steady on the boardwalk, his bootheels echoed a rhythmic beat.

A man Kate recognized as Sheriff Gentry opened the office door and stuck his head out. "Goddamnit, Harry! Your pacing is driving me batty!"

Harry stopped. He looked up with a mild frown on his face. "S-sorry, Sheriff. I s-sometimes forget mys-self."

"Something going on at home you want to talk about?" Gentry said, still standing in the office's doorway. "Or is something else bothering you?"

A sheepish grin found Harry's lips. "Nothing really. Jusst my us-sual nerve is-s all."

Kate moved from the shadows and stepped into the street towards the two men. Her right hand casually close to the Colt on her belt.

"Sheriff Gentry?"

The Sheriff looked up with surprise in his eyes. He reached for the knife fastened to his leg.

Kate said, "I'm here with a peace offering."

Harry stepped from the boardwalk onto the dusty street. He separated himself from Gentry to make it harder for a lone gunman to shoot both men.

The move surprised Kate. It was expert and precise, something she wouldn't expect from a lawman in a rathole like Unity. In response, she held her hands up, palms out. "I'm not here for a fight. I'm Kate Blaze and you have my husband wrongly locked up for rightly killing a rapist."

Harry held his ground. He looked back at Gentry. His hand on the big revolver strapped to his belt.

The Sheriff shook his head. "Hold off, Harry." Then to Kate, "You saying your husband didn't kill Deputy Haskins?"

Kate continued walking. "I'm saying he rightly killed that raping bastard and we—you and me, Sheriff—are going to talk about it."

Sheriff Gentry chuckled. A smile grooved his night darkened face.

Kate stopped short of the boardwalk. "What's so amusing, Sheriff?"

The lawman pulled himself together and stepped across the threshold between office and boardwalk. He pulled the door open wide. "My apologies, Kate Blaze, but your reputation proceeds you. I thought what they said about you was surely exaggeration, but I was wrong."

Kate tilted her head deciding how to take the lawman's

explanation.

"You may have time to laugh and whittle away the hours, Mr. Gentry, while you wait for a writ to hang my husband with the full blessing and infallibility of the law, but while you've been waiting around doing nothing, I've done your job."

"That explains it, then."

"Explains what?"

"I expected you here much earlier, after seeing you in that alley when I took J.D. into custody."

"I see you and my husband are on a first name basis?" Kate stepped from the street to the boardwalk.

"Not exactly, ma'am. What's this about you doing my job?"

Kate gave a tight smile. A smile J.D. called her stubbornness mouth twitch. "I found the girl your deputy was attempting to rape in that alley."

"Oh? Where is she?" The Sheriff held the door wide as Kate approached.

Kate stopped short, placed her hand on the Colt. "Safe."

"Careful, are you?"

"I've heard a few things about this town and I don't know your part yet, Sheriff."

Gentry scowled. His eyes narrowed. He looked from Kate to Harry and back. "I'm an officer of the law, Mrs. Blaze. Nothing more, nothing less."

Kate nodded. "In that case, the girl J.D. saved in the alley? She's prepared to testify that J.D.'s actions were self-defense."

Sheriff Gentry rubbed his forehead with the palm of his big right hand. "You want to come in and we can talk about it?"

Kate stepped into the office. Its interior brightly illuminated with several wall mounted oil lamps. Kate's eyes watered at the smell; sweat, puke and shit mixed together in a noxious cocktail. Before she could complain, she saw a disheveled and beat-up J.D. sitting awkwardly on a broken down wooden chair. His hands manacled behind his back.

Kate said, "Jehoram Delphonso!"

Only one person in the world could call J.D. by his given name and still be standing when that last "o" left their mouth. And Kate only used it when J.D. was in big trouble.

"How could you get yourself in trouble on our wedding anniversary!"

"I'm sorry, Kate." J.D.'s blue eyes sparkled. A winsome smile crossed his cracked lips.

Heat rushed into Kate's cheeks. She moved across the narrow office and grasped J.D.'s hair in her right hand. She pulled his face up and kissed him. Then, feeling her passion rise, she released him and moved around the chair to straddle his leg. She found his lips again and drank deeply.

Sheriff Gentry, still standing near the door, said, "You two about finished?"

Kate straightened. Her legs still intermingled with J.D.'s.

J.D. laughed. "Damn, Kate. I'm glad to see you, too, but it's only been a few hours since we parted company."

Kate glared at J.D. "You should be careful, Mr. Blaze. There are other fish in the sea. I've had an offer this very night from an alabaster skinned man who has more than a passing fancy for me."

"Alabaster?"

"I'd s-stay clear of him, ma'am," Harry said as he stepped through the door. "He is-s trouble."

CHAPTER 11

The sitting room of Mrs. Teller's Victorian glowed warmly. Its carpet faded from a once vibrant purple to a now mottled brown. A handsome seascape, a Chinese junk on a golden sea occupied one wall. The portrait of a balding, chinless man looking stern hung on another.

A young woman lying full-length across the sofa's cushions looked up as first Kate and then J.D. entered the small room.

"Emma?" Kate motioned to J.D. "This is my husband."

J.D. nodded. "Ma'am."

Emma moved as if to rise from the sofa, but the elderly landlady rushed across the room and planted her hand on the girl's shoulder. "You stay right there."

Emma smiled wanly. "I don't know what I'd do without you, Mrs. Teller."

The old woman patted the girl's shoulder. She looked up at the chinless gentleman's portrait. "It's nice having someone to care for again and you've been through so much with the passing of your father."

Emma wiped a tear from her eye.

J.D. was struck by Emma's quiet beauty. Her blonde hair so pale it was nearly white and her blue eyes startling.

"Ah-hmm." Sheriff Gentry stood at the room's entrance,

his hat in hand. When he had everyone's attention he said, "Miss?"

"Missus," Mrs. Teller said. "Mrs. Stephen Wiley."

Gentry nodded to the landlady. He looked at Emma. "My name's Ira Gentry, and I'm the sheriff here in Unity." He looked around the room. His eyes stopped on a delicate flower-patterned chair in the corner. A stack of yellowing newspapers on its cushion.

Mrs. Teller blushed. She hurried over and cleared the papers from the chair. When she was done, she looked back at Gentry. "Please sit, Sheriff. I'm sorry about the mess, but we so seldom have company anymore."

The lawman sat. He looked from Kate to J.D. to Emma. "There's a few things we need to clear up."

The girl studied her dress with interest.

Kate said, "Emma, you need to tell the Sheriff what happened in the alley."

The girl nodded. "I understand."

The Sheriff leaned forward. "Well?"

"That man, the deputy. He'd been following me"—her eyes never moved from the front her dress—"for days. He never spoke to me, but he was always there somewhere."

Kate sat down on the floor cross-legged and took Emma's hand.

Emma looked up. She gave a tentative smile and continued. "I was so scared." She stopped, tear stained eyes flashed at J.D. "Then tonight. *You* saved me, Mr. Blaze."

J.D. felt self-conscious as the room's other three occupants looked at him.

He cleared his throat.

A smile on Kate's lips. "Modesty doesn't suit you, J.D."

"You're not off Saturday's hanging schedule yet," Sheriff Gentry said.

Emma gasped, brought her tiny hand to her mouth. "J.D.?"

The Sheriff shook his head. "Not likely, but I need you to tell me what happened or I may go with my gut and hang him anyway."

Kate laughed, deep and genuine.

J.D. felt desire rise and he must have leered because Kate said, "Watch it, mister."

He held his hands wide with his best, I didn't do anything, expression. All the time thinking about the private celebration he and Kate, and Kate's well-worn *Kama Sutra*, would have as soon as they could ditch the law and find their way back to the hotel. Kate, J.D. always thought, had a supernatural ability to read his mind, and at that moment he was certain when she smiled coyly, winked and, ever so subtly and more erotic than anything J.D. had ever seen, ran her tongue across her bottom lip in an inviting manner.

J.D. forced himself to ignore his wife and pay attention to the room's proceedings since his neck length depended on the tale Mrs. Wiley told Gentry. He shifted back to the girl as she recited his favorite part, the moment he saved Emma from the brutish—a word Kate would love, and a word he needed to drop into a future conversation to impress her with—deputy sheriff.

When Emma finished her story, Sheriff Gentry grunted. He looked at J.D. with something close to disappointment in his eyes. "I guess you're off the hook for killing Billy Haskins."

J.D. said, "Don't sound so excited about it, Sheriff."

Gentry glared at him. "I'm not happy about it since Haskins was my deputy and I'll have to explain why I released his killer without charges."

Kate said, "It would be best if you kept J.D.'s release to yourself until we leave town tomorrow. If you can."

The Sheriff stood and nodded to Kate. "I'll keep it quiet for now, but I'd recommend you leave before someone decides I'm wrong about J.D. and takes matters into their own hands."

Kate, still sitting on the floor, said to Emma, "Are you going to be all right?"

The girl nodded, but remained silent.

"I'll take good care of her," Mrs. Teller said.

"I bet you will, Mrs. Teller." Kate patted the girl's head gently. She turned and winked at J.D. "We need to get back to our anniversary celebration, Mr. Blaze."

J.D. held his hand to Kate and helped her off the floor with a strong hand. As he turned to leave a curious thought stopped him. "Emma?"

The girl's face pale, her hands trembling made J.D. feel miserable for leaving her and Mrs. Teller alone in the old house.

"Yes?"

"In the alley, you said something I didn't understand. Something about 'killing him'?"

Emma's face went a shade beyond pale. Her eyes blinked so rapidly J.D. could almost hear a shutter banging closed.

Kate leaned down and pulled the girl's hands into her own. "What is it, Emma? What's wrong?"

"I—" Her voice cracked. Tears burst from her eyes.

J.D. gave her a hanky from his trouser pocket. The girl took it quickly. She covered her eyes and nose with it.

Kate questioned J.D. with narrowed eyes.

"It's clean!"

Kate shook her head at J.D. and then kneeled next to

the girl. She caressed Emma's cheek with the back of her hand. "It's okay, Emma. You're safe here."

It took Emma several minutes to regain her emotions. J.D. and the Sheriff looked at paintings, carpet and ceiling patterns with a fascination neither had ever felt before. Mrs. Teller busied herself in the kitchen brewing coffee and tea. Kate simply kneeled next to the girl and cooed in her ear.

When Emma had settled herself, she said, "Deputy Haskins told me they're going to kill my husband."

Sheriff Gentry said, "Who's going to kill your husband?"

"I—" Emma stopped. She looked at Kate.

"Do you know who is going to kill Stephen?" Kate said.

The girl's head trembled. Her eyes wide with tension. She opened her mouth to speak, but closed it without any words.

Kate said, "You can tell us. We're your friends, Emma."

Emma looked from Kate to Sheriff Gentry.

"Sheriff Gentry?" J.D. said.

The girl nodded.

CHAPTER 12

J.D. made a quick move toward Gentry. His heavy steps shook the floor. "You got something that needs saying?"

The lawman raised his hands with their palms out. He stepped backwards until the wall halted his progress. "Whatever you're thinking, J.D., you're dead wrong. I'm as new in this town as Mrs. Wiley. I'd been looking for an excuse to fire Haskins since I arrived. You shooting him did me a favor."

"You have anything to do with what happened to Emma?" J.D. was so close to Gentry his spittle splashed against the other man's face. "You planning to kill her husband?"

Gentry dropped his right hand to the knife attached at his belt.

J.D. held his ground and bent his knees. His feet spread wide as he prepared for a fight.

"Hold up, Gentry." Kate eased the Colt from its leather. "You take that knife out and I'll shoot you dead."

The lawman studied Kate with hard eyes, his mouth a narrow slash, before pulling his hand away from the blade. "Okay, but I want to talk. So call off your husband."

"You heard him, J.D. Back off."

J.D. went perfectly still for several seconds. The room's

temperature seemed to rise as he studied the lawman.

"J.D.?"

The gunslinger glanced at Kate, red-hot anger stained his eyes. After what seemed like minutes Kate saw the tension leave his body and he backed away.

J.D. said, "Let's talk."

The lawman looked from J.D. to Kate. "I'm not sure what just happened."

"Good, let's talk," Kate said to J.D. She turned to Gentry, "Are you part of the gang that's planning to kill Stephen Wiley?"

Gentry grimaced. He shook his head. "That's crazy. I'd never heard of the Wileys—Emma or Stephen—before tonight."

"Bullshit," J.D. said. "Why'd Haskins call for you when I had him cornered?"

"J.D.," Kate said. "Why don't you go see if Mrs. Teller needs help in the kitchen?"

J.D. jerked his head towards Kate. "What?"

Kate motioned for J.D. to leave the room.

The big man glared at Gentry, then looked back at Kate. "Kill him if he moves."

No one spoke until J.D. disappeared around the corner.

Kate, her eyes never leaving Gentry, said to Emma, "Is that what you meant? That Gentry is part of the plan to murder your husband?"

The girl gagged on the words. "Yes. No. I—"

"I have nothing to do with this," Gentry said.

"Shut up." Kate's voice strong, then to Emma, "You don't know?"

The girl nodded. Her face taut with tension.

"Okay. We're still friends. All of us. You could have let them tear J.D. apart in that alley, Sheriff, but you didn't.

That tells me something about you. Something good. Why don't you sit down and we can talk?" Kate holstered the Colt and watched as Gentry found the flower-patterned corner chair again.

Kate turned to Emma. "Did Deputy Haskins tell you he was going to kill your husband?"

The girl whispered, "No."

"Why do you think he intended to kill your husband?"

"He— The things he said." Emma paused and looked at Kate with steady eyes. "He was excited about telling Stephen what he was doing to me."

"Raping you?"

"Yes. I'm sure he planned to kill me."

"Did he say that?"

"He whispered something about our farm. That's where Stephen is now. He's building a house for us to live in."

"What did Haskins say about it?" Kate's voice as mild as she could make it.

"He said, 'when it was done' and how much Stephen would enjoy listening to what he was doing to me, how I'd scream."

"When *what* was done?"

The girl looked at Kate in confusion. Her blue eyes the color of Colorado sky. "The farm. He said, 'when we're done with the farm.'"

Kate pushed down her pulsing anger. She turned to Gentry. "You said you where new in town, Sheriff?"

A curt nod. "I've been here six weeks."

"My feeling is you're not a small-town lawman?"

"I worked as a detective in Denver for fifteen years."

"The fellow back at your office. Where's he from?"

"Same place. His name's Harry Minor. We've worked together for years and I coaxed him to come along."

"Back at the jail, you mentioned something to me, Sheriff." J.D.'s voice startled Kate, but its tone gave her comfort that he had calmed himself. "You said something is wrong in Unity. What did you mean?"

The lawman leaned back in his chair. A mirthless grin on his face. "Something's not right. Everyone's scared and not many townspeople will talk to Harry or me."

Kate said, "Who hired you?"

"The Merchant's Committee. They pay both me and Harry. Haskins and Frank, too."

J.D. said, "What did they say about the town when you were hired?"

"They had a few concerns." Gentry moved forward in the chair, his hands went still. "A syndicate moved into town a year ago. They opened a whorehouse called the *Wanderlust* and a few hoodlums began extorting the merchants with threats to their businesses and families."

"They hired you to stop the shakedowns?"

Gentry nodded. "That and the prior sheriff went missing. He went for a ride one afternoon and never came back. The funny thing, not too long after the sheriff disappeared the shakedowns stopped."

Kate said, "They stopped? Do you think the prior sheriff had something to do with the extortion racket?"

"No idea why it stopped, but I think Sheriff Jones got a line on something and he was killed for it."

J.D. said, "What makes you think that?"

"Nothing other than intuition, I'm afraid. But something odd is going on. A week or two after I came to town Mervin Jenkins. He runs the assay shop in town, told me Sullivan and Timmons"—he turned to J.D.—"you met Sully earlier tonight at the jail."

J.D. said, "I remember."

The lawman looked back to Kate and said, "Those two brought in a gold coin. An inch around. It was stamped and weighted already, but they asked him to assay it for gold content."

"What did he find?" Kate said.

"Ninety percent."

Kate looked at J.D. with raised eyebrows.

J.D. said, "Where do you think it came from?"

"No idea, other than I'd bet a year's pay it was stolen."

"These men—"

J.D. interrupted Kate, "Sullivan and Timmons—"

Kate scowled, which silenced him in a hurry. "They were part of the extortion racket?"

Gentry nodded and cleared his throat. "They *were* the racket if what I hear is true."

"You think the shakedowns stopped because those crooks found greener pastures?" J.D. said.

"That's my guess." The lawman looked at Kate hard, his pale eyes shimmered in the lamplight. "They killed Sheriff Jones, too. Sully all but admitted it earlier tonight at the jail."

"One more question," Kate said, "why didn't you like Haskins?"

"A bit off, corrupt maybe. I never saw him do anything untoward, but he had that smell about him. Harry figured he was spying on us."

J.D. said, "You think he was in with the syndicate boys?"

Gentry stood, his hat in his right hand. "Maybe, but I don't know." He looked from Kate to J.D. and back again. "I reckon I need to ride out and see if any harm's befallen Mr. Wiley. You two want to come?"

"Sure, if it can wait till morning. It's been a long day and it's past our bedtime." J.D. winked at Kate as he said the last word.

Kate shook her head at J.D.'s presumption. "I am awfully tired."

"It'll be morning before I go," Gentry said, then to Emma, "You have a map to your property, ma'am?"

The girl nodded.

"Good," Kate said, "I know a guide we can hire."

J.D. and Gentry looked at each other, confusion in their eyes.

• • •

The room's darkness suffocated Sully. The air stale. His mouth twitched at the corner, his left foot bounced as he sat on the uncomfortable hard wooden chair across from Guggenheim. The albino's face a ghost as he leaned against the desk.

"What did our Emma tell them?"

Sully fidgeted with a seam on his shirt cuff. He coughed in his hand. Then said, "I don't know. I couldn't get close enough to the house because a kid standing out front."

"They went back to the hotel?"

Sully nodded. When Guggenheim kept quiet the second-rate gunman hurried to fill the silence. "They're leaving no time soon. I waited fifteen minutes. Their room light brightened and stayed that way."

Guggenheim's chair squeaked as he leaned back. "Does Emma know what happened to her father, I wonder?"

Sully swallowed with a loud wet clack. "Davies?"

"Who else?" Guggenheim's voice hard with scorn.

"I could kill her. The Wiley woman, if you want."

"We should assume the Blazes know we killed Davies, and why, which changes things. I think Mrs. Wiley can serve a better purpose now. Something of an insurance policy."

Sully said, "What about the Blazes?"

Guggenheim set his palms flat on the desk separating him and Sully. "As much as I admire Kate Blaze's beauty I'm afraid she and her husband must die."

"What about Gentry?"

Guggenheim said, "Him too."

Sullivan smiled. "I want Gentry for myself."

"Your enthusiasm is admirable."

CHAPTER 13

Kate nonchalantly unbuckled her gun belt. She dropped it on the hotel room's only table with a clatter. A folded newspaper under one leg almost kept it from wobbling, but it rattled against the wall. A smile spread across Kate's mouth. "I guess I should be more careful, lest I break something or wake up the neighbors."

J.D. said, "There are more pleasurable ways to wake up the neighbors."

"That's true." A wickedness flashed in Kate's dark eyes. She unfastened her shirt's top button. She teased the placket between her fingers before going to the next button and the next until the shirt opened wide. She pulled its tails from her tight denims. A pleasant wiggle inspired J.D.'s lust.

"You old lecher," Kate said as she dipped first her left shoulder and then her right to escape the shirt's grasp. It pooled calmly at her feet, but J.D. saw nothing except the miraculous jiggle of breasts held captive by the brassiere. Her pale flesh, the flat stomach widening at the hips.

J.D. said with wonder, "I'll never grow tired of you, girl."

"Hmmm." A shadow of tongue moved between her lips. She giggled with a girlish lilt. The downy blonde hair on her arms and shoulders caught the lamplight, causing a misty halo around her flesh that made her appear eternal.

J.D. felt the familiar heat. He took a tentative step towards his wife, but stopped when her hands went up.

"Not yet."

A coy cast to her jaw, a predatory gleam in her dark coffee eyes. Kate reached behind herself without looking away from J.D. After a few seconds, the brassiere fluttered to the floor, the bounce and sway of her breasts breathtaking as they fell to their natural curve. The pink nipples erect and stunning.

Kate stood straight with her shoulders back. In a sultry cadence she said, "I want your clothes off."

With shaking hands, J.D. fumbled with his shirt's buttons. When he tore it from his shoulders a button popped from its stitching and rattled across the floor. He unbuckled his belt, unfastened his fly and stepped from his trousers in a single anxious movement.

"Everything. The hat, too."

J.D. felt like a kid with Kate. The flurry of butterflies in his belly, the blood leaving his brain. He tossed his hat across the room and stepped from his underpants like they were on fire.

"I want to drink you, J.D. Live on your body, devour your soul."

J.D.'s breath caught in his throat; he ached with hard desire.

Kate lowered her hands and whispered, "Don't move." She unbuttoned her denim trousers and swiveled her hips to a rhythm only she heard and danced away from their grasp. Her toes curved to the floor and made J.D. think of the mythical. In a single smooth motion, she stepped from her dainty lace panties and left everything in a pile behind. A knowing, cat-like smile on her face, Kate loosened her ponytail, her blonde locks fell shimmering to her shoulders.

J.D.'s eyes wide with appreciation. Lust's heat blistered his crotch before rising into his belly as cold anticipation.

"Jesus," he muttered.

"Hmm," Kate responded, motioned him to the bed. "On your back."

J.D. followed Kate's instructions. He closed his eyes when she took him into her mouth and moaned with pleasure.

"I love you, Kate."

She replied with a swivel of tongue, a handful of balls, and then drew him deeper into her mouth.

After a few minutes, J.D. pulled Kate higher. He brought her lips to his and palmed her breasts. He took each nipple between two fingers and alternated from massage to pinch, while circling her areolas with his thumbs.

Kate pushed J.D. flat against the mattress and wriggled forward until her stomach rubbed against J.D.'s cock. She lifted herself onto him with a moan. A warm wave flooded J.D.'s body and as Kate began moving up and down, her breasts swinging like pendulums across his vision he felt himself loosen and explode with white hot pleasure.

J.D. pulled Kate against him and kissed her hard on the lips. When she pulled back, J.D. said, "I love you, my sweet Kate."

Kate curled into J.D.'s arm crook, her head on his chest, blonde hair splayed in disarray. A few loose strands tickled his nose.

She smiled warmly. "Happy anniversary, baby."

"The best yet," J.D. said.

"I should have made you wash up first." A teasing smile on her face.

"Water under the bridge." J.D. rolled away from Kate. He

reached for the small bedside table and came back with a flat wooden box. "I have something for you."

Kate sat on the bed, her back's curve, the line of her face made J.D. hard again. Kate smiled knowingly. "First things first, what's in the box?"

"Open it."

Kate studied the box in the room's glow. She glanced at J.D. with sparkling eyes. "When did you get this?"

"Aren't you going to open it?"

Kate smiled and carefully opened the box. Inside, a slender gold chain attached to a large diamond that refracted the room's light into shimmering rainbows. Kate's smile changed to shock and then excitement.

Her eyes misted with tears. "It's beautiful."

"I thought you might like it."

Kate gave a heartwarming little laugh. She snuggled up to J.D. and kissed him. Then she pulled the necklace from the box and held it at arms-length before latching it on her neck.

Her head resting on one hand, an elbow against the bed, Kate said, "How does it look?"

"A little underwhelming compared to the background."

Kate smiled the smile only J.D. ever saw. "This is why you abandoned me in that terrible saloon?"

J.D.'s stomach lurched. "I'm sorry. I'd meant to bring it with me, but…"

Kate gave J.D. a severe look before breaking into a smile. She pulled him close. "I love it."

J.D. smiled like a fool.

CHAPTER 14

The rising sun blistered the sky and bleached the plateau's semi-arid landscape into a melody of whites, yellows, and washed out reds and browns. The trail dropped into a shallow canyon. A twisting, torn-up dry wash at its center. The trail no more than a few weathered horseshoe prints meandering between greasewood and sage brush and juniper trees.

After a few hours the canyon's floor narrowed. The sandstone cliffs began to rise. The dirt turned from white to baked red. With the change in topography J.D. noticed images chipped into the sandstone cliff walls; square-bodied pronghorn, big horn sheep, spiraling eddies of tightening lines. Indian warriors with bows and arrows, gods or chiefs with robes and headdresses. The carved images pale against the varnished sandstone canvas. The narrow canyon a gallery of ancient art, carved by men and women long since gone.

"What is this place?" Kate said to J.D. with a whispered voice.

"It's marvelous." J.D. pulled up on his horse and whistled at Joshua and Gentry.

The two, several yards ahead, turned back to join J.D. and Kate.

Kate dismounted with a swivel and jump. She dropped the reins to hard ground and ran to a rock mural. She called to J.D. over her shoulder, "Come on!"

J.D., a smile on his face as he watched Kate climb over several small boulders like a young girl, said, "Why would I want to see rock art when I can look at you?"

Kate stopped a few feet shy of the mural. She turned to face J.D., each foot on a different rock. Her left hand on her hip, the other pointed straight at J.D. like a gun. "You better not be leering again, buster."

"I can't help myself."

Gentry pivoted from his saddle and followed Kate to the cliff. "I've heard about this place, but seeing it is something else entirely."

"Joshua!" Kate said.

The boy, his horse already abandoned on the trail, was a few feet behind Kate. When he responded, Kate jumped.

J.D. laughed.

Kate said, "Did your tribe make these?"

Joshua shook his head. "No, Mrs. Kate. The ancient ones made these drawings."

Gentry studied, his face close to the stone surface, what appeared to be the bastard child of a giraffe and a pronghorn. After a moment, he said to Joshua, "What do these mean?"

"No one knows, sir."

"Are they stories?" Kate wondered aloud.

J.D., still seated on his horse, said, "I bet you're right, Kate. Successful hunts, pleased gods and full bellies."

Kate traced a spiraling line cut in the stone's surface with her finger. "It's carved right in the rock. The artist is dead, but not this. *This* is still here, telling us something important. But something we're not smart enough to understand."

Joshua beamed at Kate's words. "My uncle says these are our ancestor's stories."

Kate patted the boy's head. "They're beautiful, Joshua. Is your uncle at Fort Duchesne?"

The boy shook his head. His bottom lip quivered. "No, Mrs. Kate."

"Where is he?"

Joshua stared at the rock art. He shrugged his narrow shoulders.

Sheriff Gentry, not catching the boy's mood, said, "These ancient people, they're Ute Indians?"

Joshua turned away from the rock. A smile found his face again. "No. Much older. As old as the wind, my friend says. As old as the sky. As the stars."

J.D. said, "Does that mean you don't know how old?"

Joshua giggled.

Kate raised her eyebrows. J.D. knew she wanted to keep after Joshua about his uncle, but he shook his head. Kate grimaced, but kept her tongue.

A black bird circled in the sky above. It foiled upwards on the warm air. A lizard darted across the rock. Its flint colored skin a shadow.

Silence settled on the small group.

Finally, Kate said, "I feel like I'm trespassing."

The lawman, his eyes on Joshua, said, "A special place, I think. You should be proud of it."

The boy lifted his gaze from the ground and smiled shyly.

"We better keep moving if we want to reach Wiley's place before dark," J.D. said.

Kate led the group back to their horses. She pulled a drum canteen from her saddle and offered it to Joshua and

Gentry. They both took a pull before Kate gave her horse several cupped handfuls and replaced the cap and reattached it to her saddle.

J.D. said, "None for me?"

Kate grinned; a little devil in it. "I didn't think you needed any since you didn't get off your ass."

J.D. glared, a smile in his eyes, and pulled his own canteen from its pouch. He took a steady pull, then smacked his lips. "Mine's better anyway." Then to Joshua, "How far to the, what was it? *Ames' Star*?"

"*Ames-Moon Stagecoach Inn*, J.D.," Kate said.

"One hour, Mr. J.D."

"I'm not a 'mister,' Joshua, just call me J.D."

Kate said, "A few other names come to mind, but we save those for when he's out of ear-shot."

J.D. grunted. He dismounted his horse and gave it water. "You all ready?"

With Joshua in the lead the quartet moved farther into the canyon. Its floor continued to narrow and its walls grew taller, blocking the sun. The trail cast in shadow. There were several rock falls—splintered sandstone spires—crumbled on the narrow canyon floor.

•••

Three men rode above, slashing across the plateau's surface. Dust rising in their wake, sparkled white in the late-morning sun. The horses frothy with exertion as they made their way to the small outpost midway between Unity and the Ute Reservation. The man named Sullivan in the lead, Frank steady on his heels and the third man, a stranger, riding a large roan at the rear. The natural sounds drowned by thundering hooves, snorting, overworked horses, the squeak of leather.

CHAPTER 15

Joshua stopped a few yards from where the trail narrowed to a small opening, a steep canyon wall on one side, a red rock spire on the other. Kate urged her horse forward at a slow walk. Her eyes and ears alert for any unusual sounds. She pulled up next to Joshua and said, "Where are we?"

Joshua pointed to the narrow passage. "It's through there, Mrs. Kate."

J.D. and Gentry left their horses in the trail and approached Kate and Joshua on foot. J.D.'s spurs jangled in the afternoon's stillness, Gentry's denim trousers whisked with each step.

"Well?" J.D. said.

Kate swiveled from her saddle. She pulled her well-trained horse to the trail's edge and left it ground-tied before walking back to where the men had gathered. "Joshua says the *Ames-Moon* is down slope from here. I'm going to reconnoiter"—Kate smiled as J.D. raised an eyebrow—"It means, 'look around,' J.D."

"I know what it means, but I had hoped to save it for some dark moment when I needed to impress you."

Gentry looked from J.D. to Kate and back again. "You two are plain odd."

"J.D. is an odd duck, Sheriff, but a good bird nonetheless."

Joshua joined the group.

J.D. looked at the boy, tousled his hair with his big right hand. "Gentry said, 'you two'; as in both of us, Kate. Me *and* you."

Kate placed her hand on J.D.'s shoulder. "I heard, but chose to interpret its exact meaning."

Gentry shook his head, chuckling. "You two need time to figure this out?"

A glimmer shone in J.D.'s eyes, he opened his mouth to speak, but Kate beat him. "Don't say what you're thinking, J.D."

The boy laughed, hands on his belly, until tears started streaming down his face.

"You think this is pretty funny, do you?"

Joshua straightened. "Yes, ma'am. You and J.D. are exactly like the books make you out to be."

Kate gave J.D. a headshake and a stern look, knowing his low opinion of the unauthorized yellow-back *Blaze!* tales sold across the country and purporting to be based on factual happenings.

J.D. scratched his three-day beard and winked at Kate. "You know, Joshua. You shouldn't believe anything you read. That goes double for anything with an exclamation point in its title."

Joshua's eyes narrowed with bewilderment, then widened with a pleased understanding. "Like *Blaze!*?"

"Exactly."

Kate shook her head, smiling. "If we're done with the horse play, I have a proposal. I'm going to peek past that narrow passage. I want you three to stay here. If you hear any trouble I expect a hasty rescue. Do you think you can do that?"

Joshua said, "Yes, Mrs. Kate."

The two men nodded.

• • •

Kate moved through the narrow entrance. The cliff walls tailed away to reveal a sun soaked valley surrounded on one side by varnished sandstone and on the other by broken white stone and dirt rising to a tabletop plateau. The change from varnished red to pale white stunned Kate's senses. She blinked at the brightness, brought her hands over her eyes.

Kate studied the valley floor. The landscape bland and dry. An empty wash with its jagged bank rising above a seemingly flat bottom, curled along the far canyon wall. Three small rectangular stone buildings crowded to the sandstone on the valley's left side. The trail widened around the buildings before narrowing again and continuing its march northward.

A corral against the varnished sandstone held five dusky red horses. A wide and low stone barn at one end. A bunkhouse at the other. At the front, forming a misshapen triangle with the other buildings, sat a large two-story house, glass windows, a porch running along its wide face.

The small enclave of buildings appeared deserted. Nothing moved in the yard or the surrounding valley.

"Looks quiet as the grave."

Kate jumped, startled by J.D.'s voice.

"Damn you, J.D. Blaze! You scared me half to death."

J.D. rubbed Kate's back with his palm, which she took as an apology. "We sure anybody's here?"

"I'm not sure of anything, but there are horses in the corral." Kate's eyes taking in the plateau's baked white rim on the valley's western edge. "It is mighty quiet."

"Let's find out." J.D. whistled and Gentry appeared, trailed by his and J.D.'s horses. Joshua followed with his paint and Kate's horse.

Kate said, "We going to ride straight in?"

"Yeah, but be watchful since I have a bad feeling about this place."

"Me too," Kate said.

J.D. led the small group into the valley. Kate dropped back to the rear as protection against an ambush, Gentry and Joshua at the center. The clop of hooves. Dust rising with each step, a rattling snake's tail in the distance, the quartet's only accompaniment.

But everything changed when Kate saw lightning flash, dirt geyser close to J.D.'s horse. Thunder hammered across the valley. The scene moved in slow motion; the horse reared back with fright, J.D. lost the saddle and seemed to hang in the air for minutes before slamming to the ground with a thud.

The world came back to speed and chaos erupted.

CHAPTER 16

J.D. twisted in the air to his left as his horse bucked. His intention was to clear the terrified animal and land on his feet, but J.D. misjudged the distance to the ground, over-rotated and took the impact on his left hip and lower back. His head snapped and bounced with a meaty thud on the hard ground. Stars exploded in his vision, faded in a narrowing black circle. He opened and closed his eyes trying to will away unconsciousness, his jaw worked itself wide, refused to close.

J.D. tried to breathe, but his lungs refused air. He gasped. His head throbbed. His thoughts confused and jumbled. He knew a shot had been fired, but not from where. The shooter could be a few feet or yards away. J.D. pushed himself up on an elbow. The fine dust burrowing into his mouth. He forced himself to relax and worked his lungs with wheezy, ragged breaths.

He rose to his feet and pulled the large bore Colt from its cross-draw rig. The white velvety dust stunted his vision, made his eyes water. A helplessness settled on him; fear rising with raised voices, shouts, horses rushing across flat ground. A harsh buzz in his ears. His eyes saw only white trimmed in ragged black, throbbing in and out with each heartbeat.

J.D. moved on liquid legs. His knees wobbled, head pounding. The world swirled around him. The .44 at arm's length. Its barrel unsteady, J.D.'s finger pressed tight against the trigger guard as he looked for a target.

Chaos erupted around him as his head began to clear. Indecipherable shouts. The crack and boom of gunshots. J.D. moved forward, still blinded by dust and pain. He stopped with every step to keep from falling. The fog-like dust began to settle and drift back to the ground. J.D.'s horse a ghost as it galloped across the valley toward the ranch house and corral. Gentry, standing next to his horse, a long gun across its saddle aimed high on the plateau, fired, levered another round into the chamber and fired again.

A hand roughly grabbed J.D.'s elbow and pulled. He jerked away and swung around with his Colt extended, finger on the trigger.

"It's me!" Kate lurched backwards, her hands raised in the air.

J.D. dropped his gun hand to his side. "I nearly killed you, Kate."

Kate stepped close to J.D. and cupped her hand over his ear. "We need to get over there." She pointed toward jumbled white sedimentary slabs fifty feet down trail.

J.D. stood still, trying to keep his feet on the swirling ground.

Kate stepped past him. She pulled the Winchester to her shoulder, aimed, and fired another shot toward the plateau. When she turned back, concern in her eyes, she said, "You okay, J.D.?"

J.D. shook his head and pain blistered his skull. He stumbled and fell to a knee before Kate grabbed his arm. She steadied him then slapped his face.

"You're not leaving me, J.D. Not now. We need to get into those rocks and I can't carry you."

J.D. blinked.

He looked at the Colt in his hand and shakily replaced it in the holster.

"Help me up."

Kate retrieved her Winchester from where she had dropped it, placed a shoulder inside J.D.'s arm and lifted. The two staggered, but kept their feet. A dirt geyser jumped a few feet away from a bullet's impact.

"We need to hurry," Kate said. Then she shouted to Gentry over her shoulder, "Cover us!"

Gentry's response was an ear-splitting rifle shot.

Another geyser erupted from solid ground no more than a yard away. Then another.

Kate twisted back and triggered her rifle at the plateau. She levered a fresh round with one hand while helping J.D. walk with the other.

J.D.'s head cleared with each step. His legs strengthened. The pain still alive, but the shock and darkness ebbing.

J.D. pushed Kate away. "I can make it."

Kate looked at his eyes. A scowl on her face as she studied her husband. She nodded after a moment and released J.D.

She moved a few steps away and dropped a knee in the dirt. Kate pulled the rifle to her shoulder and fired. She worked the lever, the spent casing flipped upwards and away, its brass flashing sunlight. A fresh round slammed into the chamber.

Kate sighted down the barrel and fired again.

J.D. dropped behind a boulder. His back against its warm surface, his butt on the ground. He pulled the .44

from his cross-draw rig, twisted so he could see Kate.

"Your turn!"

Kate shot again. She levered her rifle.

"Gentry!" Kate shouted.

The lawman, lying prone behind his now dead horse, pounded bullets toward the shooter. He waved his hand at Kate without looking back and fired another shot, then racked a fresh round into his rifle.

Kate ran toward the rock field. Her knees bent. A flash appeared from a vertical shadow near the plateau's ridgeline. Dirt splashed a few feet behind Kate, the explosive report echoed across the valley.

J.D. aimed and fired his Colt. He thumbed back the hammer and fired again. The long shot made J.D. wish for his rifle still attached to his saddle. Another flame popped from the dark shadow, a whine sizzled past J.D.'s head, sparked rock several feet behind him.

J.D. threw another round at the shooter.

Kate moved into the rocks in a hurry. She tumbled between two slabs and using the rock as support for her Winchester smashed more lead into the plateau.

J.D. said, "Where's Joshua?"

Kate pointed across the valley to the plateau's base where the boy was lying flat, his face a few inches from the ground as he examined his surroundings.

"Is he hurt?"

"No!"

A bullet whistled past. J.D. and Kate instinctively ducked below the rocks.

Kate's flat-brimmed hat lopsided on her head, face slick with sweat, eyes squinting against the desert light.

"He's serious."

"There are at least two shooters." Kate lifted her head

high enough to see over the rocks and pulled her Colt from its leather and fired in a single smooth motion.

"How do you know?"

"One man would need to reload sometime, but these bastards have their timing down." She fired another hopeless shot with her Colt. "We need to get Gentry over here."

J.D. crawled to the boulder field's edge and crouched below a long flat stone, cupped his hands around his mouth, "Gentry!"

The lawman fired another round and levered a fresh load. He turned his head to J.D.

J.D. motioned Gentry over with his right arm.

Gentry hollered a war cry, or cursed. J.D. couldn't decipher exactly what.

Kate returned to her long rifle. She fired as quickly as she could pull the trigger and rack fresh lead.

The lawman pulled down tight to the ground before pushing up from behind his dead horse. His legs moved like steam pistons. His rifle held low in his right hand.

J.D. and Kate fired at the shadow darkened cliff hiding the sniper.

A cry of wounded animal pain caught J.D.'s attention. Gentry tumbled forward. A red halo shimmered in the afternoon light.

Kate rose from her cover and started toward the Sheriff. Another bullet slammed into the ground next to the lawman, dirt cascaded over his prostrate form.

J.D. shouted, "Kate, no!"

CHAPTER 17

Kate jumped onto the boulder's flat surface. Her boots slippery on the smooth stone. The bootheels clacking as she ran to the fallen lawman. She switched the Winchester from her right hand to the left, palming the fore stock with a tight grip and drew the Colt from its leather and fired off two rounds before it clacked on a spent shell. She re-holstered the Colt as she moved from the boulder field and across the ten feet separating her and Gentry.

Dirt exploded so close Kate felt it against her arm and face. She dropped into a slide a few feet from the wounded man. She spun tightly so her feet swung wide and her upper body matched up with Gentry's. The lawman perfectly still, his face in the dirt, pooling blood beneath his right shoulder.

Kate feared him dead.

She placed a finger against the artery in his neck and felt the reassuring pulse of life. She rolled onto her side, towards J.D. where he was firing his Colt at their hidden sniper, shouted his name. When he looked she hefted her rifle in the air and motioned her intent to throw it to him.

J.D. nodded, shouted something stolen from Kate's ears by the echoing booms.

Kate worked her rifle's lever, ejected the live round,

pushed the incoming shell down and closed the rifle's action on an empty chamber. She palmed the barrel in her right hand, used her left as a guide and tossed it underhanded. The rifle landed a few feet from J.D.

J.D. yanked the Winchester from the hardpan soil. He checked the barrel for a blockage and racked a fresh load into the chamber and began shooting.

Kate, on her knees, pulled Gentry on to his back. A large open wound oozed blood from his shoulder below the collar bone. His eyes flickered open, a smile brushed past his mouth.

"Leave me, Kate."

"Hell, no."

Kate moved so she was behind Gentry's head and shoulders. She grabbed him under both arms and pulled him toward the boulder field. The lawman groaned. Kate felt the air pressure sizzle as a bullet spun close. A hair-raising crackle in its wake. She ducked lower and pulled harder on Gentry. The lawman bicycling with his legs to help Kate move him.

Pain blistered across Kate's right arm.

She released Gentry and stumbled backward. The bullet's heavy impact twisted her sideways. She nearly crashed down on her back, but with her left hand she stopped the fall; pain blossomed across her shoulder, prickled down her arm and into her wrist and hand. Ignoring the wound Kate rose to her knees, grasped Gentry and pulled again.

A heavy hand on Kate's uninjured shoulder tugged her off-balance and then two strong hands dragged her backwards. She looked up into J.D.'s face. When she was in the boulder field's safety, J.D. went back for Gentry and pulled him into the rocks. J.D. dropped down next to Kate.

His breathing ragged, a smile on his face. The valley quiet except for the steady buzz in Kate's ears and the arcing pain on her right side.

"Goddamn," J.D. said. "Who the hell are those guys?"

Kate laughed.

Gentry said, "Whoever it is sure doesn't like you two."

"Us? What about you?" Kate said.

"I've been Sheriff for six weeks and nobody's taken a shot at me before you showed up." The lawman coughed and then cursed.

Kate crawled over to the Winchester leaning against the rock, looked longingly at Gentry's abandoned rifle lying where he had fallen.

J.D. said to Kate. "You okay?"

"It clipped me." She looked at her arm, her sleeve torn at an angle. Blood leeched from a wound burned black by the passing bullet. "But it hurts like hell."

J.D. applied pressure to Gentry's wound. "It looks clean, Sheriff."

"It doesn't feel clean."

J.D. laughed. "You'll live."

Kate, her back against the stone, pushed bullets into the Winchester's loading port. When it was fully stocked, she rolled onto her knees and looked up at the shadow hiding the snipers. The valley's sudden silence unnerving. When she found no obvious target, Kate looked over at Joshua still prostrate on the ground at the cliff's base and waved.

The boy smiled, waved back.

Kate blushed with admiration for Joshua. She motioned for him to stay down. He nodded with vigor.

Kate searched the plateau's broken wall for movement, for anything to drop a bead on and crash a bullet through. The ambush made her angry as hell. J.D. smashed up,

Gentry taking a bullet. His horse lying dead. A feeling of Old Testament vengeance rising.

She wasn't a gleeful killer. It happened in her and J.D.'s business, but she never looked forward to it, took pride in it, and certainly didn't enjoy it. But at that moment she wanted nothing more than to wreak havoc on the cowardly men who set the ambush. Punish them for their wanton cold-blooded lust to kill. But mostly she wanted to protect her friends. J.D., Joshua and Sheriff Gentry. But damn if revenge wasn't part of the deal.

Kate surveyed the plateau. The rifle moved with her gaze, an extension of her person. In her peripheral vision, she saw J.D. rush from behind the cover and onto the open valley floor. Her heart seemed to stop, but her vigilance never wavered. She knew he was going after Gentry's rifle and it scared her badly.

Sunlight on blued steel caught Kate's attention. The shooter still invisible, Kate lined up the shot where she imagined the man holding the weapon would be. She drew a breath, exhaled and pulled the trigger. The Winchester bucked, smoke belched, as the explosion pushed the bullet towards the plateau's edge.

A primal scream.

A stream of curses as a man appeared from the depression, stepped forward and fell from the plateau's face. He bounced against the steep hillside twice before disappearing behind a low-rising foothill a hundred yards from where Kate knelt.

She moved her focus from the plateau to where she had last seen J.D. and sighed with relief as he moved back into the broken field with Gentry's rifle in his hands. She turned her attention back to the hillside and scanned for another target.

A rifle's report made Kate flinch because it came from behind. She pivoted toward the gunshot. The Winchester steady in her hands. Three men moved across the valley toward her small group, each held a rifle in his hands. Kate put a bead on the first man, flaming red hair on his head. And eased her finger onto the trigger.

CHAPTER 18

"Put down your guns!" The redhead shouted. His rifle ready at his shoulder, but its muzzle pointed at the ground.

J.D. analyzed the situation and decided hesitation was in their best interest.

"Hold up, Kate."

Kate looked at J.D. Her rifle steady and on target. She frowned, opened her mouth as if she had something to say, but closed it again before nodding her agreement.

"Come out of there," Red Hair said. "Your hands empty."

"We have a wounded man," J.D. shouted without leaving cover. "And there is at least one bastard on the plateau wanting to ventilate us."

Red Hair lowered the rifle from his shoulder. His right hand in the lever and his left on the fore stock so he could get it back to firing position in a hurry. "He skedaddled. You're safe to come out."

"Okay." J.D. scooted to where Kate kneeled, hunched over her rifle. "What do you think?"

Kate responded without taking her hand off the Winchester. "I'm uneasy about it, but my instincts are always blurred after a shoot-out."

J.D. nodded. "You're okay with us moving from cover, then?"

"Yeah." Kate lowered her rifle. "I guess I am."

J.D. said, "We're coming out. But we're not dropping our guns. We won't shoot if you don't."

Red Hair looked at his companions, each grimaced in turn and nodded. They didn't bother to put any distance between themselves and that made J.D. feel good about their intentions. Or, if they were hired guns, their incompetence.

Red Hair said, "That'll be fine."

To Kate, J.D. said, "I'm going to show myself. You mind putting a bead back on the plateau since we *know* those bastards want to kill us?"

Kate swiveled to the narrow trench's other side. She pulled the Winchester to her shoulder and put its front bead on the shadow where the men had been hiding.

"Okay."

J.D. stood to reveal his upper body to the three men. Gentry's rifle held firmly in his hands. He counted to ten, trying not to show his desire to flinch as he waited for a bullet to slam into his chest or back. When nothing happened he turned to Kate, "Anything?"

"Quiet as death."

"Not the word I wanted to hear." Then to the three men, "I'm going to walk over this way"—he pointed down the narrow rock alley to his left—"and exit there."

Red Hair nodded.

J.D. moved to the boulder field's edge. He stepped over Gentry, winked at the lawman. He stopped a few feet outside the protective stone labyrinth. "We have a wounded man here. His name's Ira Gentry and he's the sheriff in Unity. We need some help moving him."

"Tell the other rifleman to come out, then we'll help you with the lawman."

J.D. grimaced at Red Hair's referral to Kate as a 'rifle*man*' since he knew it would make her angry.

"Come on, Kate."

The three men looked at each other, a small wiry fellow wearing spectacles and a yellow shirt said, "Kate?"

Kate stood, a frown on her face. "You better believe it's 'Kate.'"

"No offense meant, ma'am," said the man. His two friends laughed at his obvious discomfort.

Kate nodded, her mouth a line. "Some taken." She followed J.D.'s path through the boulder field and stopped where Gentry was lying and kneeled beside his prone figure. "How are you, Ira?"

"I'll survive." He snuck a peek at J.D. and his eyes returned to Kate. "It's been a long time since anyone as pretty as you called me 'Ira.'"

Kate smiled, tousled his hair with her hand. "Where's your hat?"

A thin smile on his lips. "Damn if I know."

Kate removed her flat-brimmed hat, placed it on Gentry's head. "Till we find yours." She stepped over the lawman, her blonde hair shimmering in the desert sun, and walked from the boulder field. The Colt in its leather. The Winchester in her right hand.

J.D.'s heart pounded like a thirteen-year-old boy, his mouth dry as a desert, as he watched her swivel towards him, a smile on her face. He remembered where they were, shook his head and shamed himself for indulging fantasy.

Kate turned to the plateau, gave a "come here" motion to the prone boy, said, "Joshua."

Red Hair's eyes bulged. He made a nervous motion with his rifle and brought it to his shoulder.

J.D. held his hand up, palm out. "Wait. Joshua's an

Indian boy helping us find Stephen Wiley's place. He isn't armed and he's no threat to you. Hell"—J.D. grinned broadly—"none of us are a threat to you."

Red Hair lowered his rifle when he saw Joshua. The boy approached Kate and J.D., his eyes looking at the ground, his hands in his pockets. When he arrived, Kate gave him a hug, held him back by his shoulders, said, "How are you, handsome?"

The boy's face paled, a tear popped from his eye.

J.D., grinning like a teenager, said, "Kate, this is too much. First you flirt with Gentry. Hell, you give him the hat I bought you on your birthday. And now it's Joshua. I'm not a jealous man, but this is taking it too far."

Joshua looked from J.D. to Kate. A giggle escaped and turned quickly to raucous laughter. He bent over, hands on knees, and laughed away the stresses from the last several minutes.

"This is no laughing matter," J.D. said to keep the game going.

Kate said, "If you can't tolerate a modern woman's desires, Mr. Blaze, you best keep riding and let me be."

The three men looked at each other, the uneasiness on their faces replaced with hesitant mirth. The small man with spectacles slapped Red Hair on the back. The two looked at each other and laughed.

"Hey!" Gentry shouted. "I'm shot."

J.D. looked at Kate. The most beautiful smile he'd ever seen on her face.

"We better go help the lawman."

J.D. said, "I guess."

CHAPTER 19

Red Hair was James Ames and Spectacles was Moses Moon, both middle aged with a lifetime under the blistering desert sun. Crow's feet crinkled around their eyes and their faces were stained and marked by wind and heat and cold. The two men formed the partnership of Ames-Moon. The third, a stocky man in his thirties with a cherub face, was introduced only as Billy. He looked like a stable hand; his boots stained yellow-green and his trousers filthy. He smelled bad. His eyes cast shyly at the ground.

It took Gentry a few minutes to gain his feet, but once he did he was able to walk and he refused help.

J.D. with a mischievous grin on his face, said, "What if Kate helped?"

"Well," Gentry said, returning J.D.'s grin, "everyone needs help sometime."

Kate offered a shoulder, but Gentry politely turned her down.

The horses were scattered. J.D.'s and Joshua's standing by the corral. Kate's had retreated down the trail and Gentry's was dead. James Ames sent Billy after Kate's horse and everyone else walked towards the buildings. Gentry a little slow, but he moved better than J.D. expected.

When they reached the house, identified with a small painted sign as the *Ames-Moon Stagecoach Inn*, James Ames invited them in. J.D. stopped a few steps from the door, asked Joshua to look after the horses.

Moses Moon with high-pitched voice said, "Put them in the corral."

"Yes, sir." Joshua sprinted to where his and J.D.'s horses loitered.

"Maybe we should keep him," J.D. said to Kate. "I'm starting to like the boy. He's helpful."

Kate frowned. "Sure. Maybe next time he'll get shot."

J.D. was smart enough to keep his tongue. He raised his hands in surrender and watched Kate pivot away and walk into the hotel with a tight gait. Her ponytail bounced angrily with each step. He was in trouble, but wasn't sure why since the two had been in tighter situations than they now faced. And more than once.

The building's fine interior surprised J.D. The walls papered with a tasteful flowered pattern. A feminine hand obvious in its choice. A narrow pine desk disguised as oak at the room's back wall. A large dinner table to the right. An open staircase traveled across the back wall from the first floor to second.

"Have a seat," James said, as he pulled a chair away from the table and sat down.

"What about Gentry and Kate?"

"Moses will see to them in the back room."

J.D. nodded. "Nice place."

"Thank you."

"What I can't figure is why it's here. No stage route anywhere and the trail we followed wouldn't accommodate a coach anyway."

Ames shifted uncomfortably in his chair. "My wife left a

few months ago with the sentiment."

J.D. said, "I figured a woman was behind these papered walls."

Ames looked at his hands. When he looked back at J.D. his eyes brimmed red. "The Army's been promising a road between Unity and Fort Duchesne for years. Me and Moses purchased the land and built the hotel. We were hoping for a windfall, but instead we're going broke."

"No idea when the road's coming?"

"None," excitement touched Ames' voice now, "but this place sits on the highest groundwater between Unity and Fort Duchesne. It's the only logical place for a trail station. Once that road's built we'll make money hand over fist. The Army and anybody else traveling will pay for feed and water and some will even buy a room."

"Nice deal." J.D. put his elbows on the table and leaned forward. "We're looking for a farmer named Stephen Wiley. You know him?"

Ames leaned back in his chair. His sales pitch and the subject change seemed to improve his mood. "You a relation?"

J.D. shook his head. "I know his wife. She's afraid someone is trying to kill him."

Ames studied J.D. a moment before he answered. "I've seen him a few times. Keeps to himself. Doesn't much look like a farmer. A city man, if I've seen one."

"Where's his place?"

"Not far. Maybe four miles as the crow flies." Ames shifted in his chair, straightened. "He doesn't really have a place. Lives in a tent. The last time I was out there it didn't look he planned to build a cabin any time soon."

"What's he doing if he's not building?"

The two men looked over as Kate walked into the room

and pulled a chair away from the table and sat down.

Ames nodded, said, "Mrs. Blaze—"

"Kate." She looked at J.D., smoldering anger still in her eyes.

"Kate." Ames turned back to J.D. "No idea what Wiley's doing out there."

"Farming?" J.D. said.

"Nothing at all usual for a homesteader. No buildings, no crops. Visitors pass by here routinely. Not sure if they're invited since we don't get over there much and he's not friendly towards us."

Kate said, "Who visits him?"

"Well." Ames looked uncomfortable under Kate's scrutiny and J.D. didn't blame him. "They're secretive. They don't travel on the main trail, but come over the plateau. That trail drops into the valley half a mile north. We can hear them clomping a few miles out."

"Why's it odd to use the plateau?"

"It's a hell of a trail. Nobody takes it unless they don't know where they're going."

J.D. looked at Kate. The anger still in her eyes, but now it was accompanied by curiosity.

"Why would Wiley have guests at his place?" Kate said.

J.D. turned to Ames. "You know the men?"

Ames looked at his hands. They were clasped together on the table's surface. "One is familiar."

J.D. waited several seconds, when it became clear James Ames had no intention to continue, he said, "Who?"

The hotel keeper looked scared; skin chalky, a slight tremor in his hands.

"Well?" Kate said.

The air seemed heavier while J.D. and Kate watched Ames. The silence thicker. Kate tapped the fingers on the table. Her nails clacked louder and louder.

"That albino." The words came from Moon, who leaned against the doorjamb at the back of the room. J.D. hadn't seen him enter.

Ames turned quickly to Moon's voice. "You sure this is what we want to do?"

The little man shook his head. "No, but it's what we *should* do. Hell, it's probably in our best interest anyway."

"Albino?" J.D. looked between the two men.

"Marcus Guggenheim," Kate said.

"That's him. Mean sonofabitch," Ames said.

"Ugly as hell, too." This voice belonged to Sheriff Gentry. His right arm in a sling. "He runs whores out of the *Wanderlust* in Unity."

"You know him?" J.D. said to Kate, confusion in his voice.

Kate nodded. "We met in *Petey's* last night while you were out running errands. I've seen him a few times since. I think he's been following me."

"You think was the one shooting at us?"

"Maybe," Gentry said. "But more likely it was his hired goons."

J.D. said, "Does this make sense to you Sher—"

At that moment Joshua crashed through the hotel's front door and skidded to a halt a few feet from the table. His face red, chest heaving as if he'd run a long distance. His eyes scarlet with terror.

"Joshua? What's wrong?" Kate said.

CHAPTER 20

Joshua grappled for breath. His hands on his knees. His head down. After a few moments he looked up, his eyes wet and red, and said, "It's Mr. Billy."

James Ames was the first to stand. "There's something wrong with Billy?"

Joshua nodded. A tear bubbled in his eye.

"Where is he?"

Joshua looked at Kate. "He—"

Kate moved to the boy, placed her hands on his shoulders. "What happened, Joshua?"

"They—they. I think he's dead, Mrs. Kate."

Ames rushed past Kate. His shoulder collided with hers. She lost her balance, took a step to keep from falling and bumped against Joshua. The boy stumbled, off balance. As he started to tumble backwards Kate clutched his wrist in her hand, but Joshua's momentum pulled both into a heap on the floor.

Kate stood, checked that Joshua was unhurt, and followed Ames out the front door. The afternoon glare blinded her. The sun's light reflected from the powdery white soil like it was unblemished tin.

"Kate!" The voice J.D.'s, but Kate didn't respond. Instead she cupped her hands over her eyes and looked for Ames.

"Ames!" Kate shouted when she saw him sprinting across the flat valley floor. An unmoving, prostrate man his destination. Kate's horse in the background wandering nervously across the lonesome trail. She slipped the .44 from its leather, its wood grips cool in her hand, scanned the horizon for any movement in the valley. Trail dust marked three men moving north in a hurry.

She looked over her shoulder at J.D., shouted, "Three riders!"

J.D. waved her forward. "Go!"

Kate hurried after Ames. When she arrived at the scene, Ames had already pulled Billy onto his back. The man's eyes wide. A gaping wound across his neck where a blade had been pulled across.

Ames slapped Billy lightly on each cheek. He did it again and again, whispering Billy's name over and over.

"He's dead, James." Kate holstered the Colt and kneeled beside the grieving man. After a moment, she pulled him away from Billy. James grasped her, his tears wet against her face.

"Goddamn them." He repeated again and again.

Kate held him tight, felt his body spasm with grief. She patted his back in the same manner she would settle a baby. "It's okay. You're okay."

J.D. touched her gently on the shoulder before moving to the dead man. He crouched, looked at the gruesome wound. His shoulders slumped. With his right hand he closed Billy's eyes, pulled a bandanna from his back pocket and placed it over Billy's face.

He stood, looked at Kate. A hard glint in his eyes. "They have Emma and her husband."

Kate blinked, surprise taking her breath. "What?"

"They gave Joshua a message. Emma and Stephen Wiley

are their prisoners."

"Emma? How?" Kate was stunned by the new circumstances.

"I don't know, but—"

"Mrs. Kate!" Joshua halted a few feet away. "Is he okay, Mrs. Kate?"

Ames pulled away from Kate. "I'm sorry, Kate. I'm really sorry." He stood, his back to Billy. His eyes cast a distant stare. "Billy didn't deserve this."

Kate shook her head. "No, James. Billy didn't deserve this."

"We need to bury him," Ames said to himself. "He'd want a tree in sight." He looked around the desolate valley, studied the greasewood and sagebrush at the western mesa's base. His gaze settled on something unseen to Kate. He pointed. "Over there, I think."

Kate followed his hand's direction to a cottonwood copse hidden in a depression at the mesa's sandstone base.

J.D. approached Ames, placed a hand on his shoulder. "Sure. We'll bury him in the shade of the cottonwoods."

"What about Emma, J.D.?" Kate said, back on her feet.

J.D., an uncomfortable look to the way he stood with hunched shoulders and his hands at his sides, said, "They wanted Joshua to relay a message. Emma and her husband will be killed if we dig any deeper into their private business."

"What business?" Kate said. "We have no idea what's happening around here."

J.D. shook his head.

Kate studied the horizon. The plateau's washed out yellows, browns and whites. The mesa's painted red rock. J.D.'s hesitance bothered her. The way he stood. His even, too calm manner. Even more bothersome was his lack of enthusiasm for the chase.

Kate looked at J.D. "You're not telling me something."

J.D. played his boot toe in the dirt, tracing a small circle over and over. It reminded Kate of a little boy. She wanted to cry for a reason she didn't understand.

"J.D.?"

Joshua stepped to Kate, took her hand. His eyes dry. "Mr. J.D. is frightened for you."

"For me?" She stared at the boy for a moment, waiting for him to answer. When he didn't she looked at her husband. A man with a reputation for fearlessness. A gunfighter. An adventurer. Her lover. "I don't understand."

J.D. said, "The albino offered us another deal. He'll release Emma in exchange for you."

Kate's skin crawled, her neck prickled. "That dirty bastard." Red hot anger flared. Suffocating in its intensity. She turned to Joshua. His eyes glimmering with tears again. "Did he say when and where?"

The boy looked at J.D., but Kate pulled his face back to her with gentle fingers. "Don't look at him, look at me. Where and when?"

"Kate."

"You stay out of this for a minute, J.D." She kept her eyes solidly locked on Joshua's. "Well?"

"The Wiley place, Mrs. Kate."

"When?"

J.D. said, "Before sunset."

Kate pulled a railroad watch from a pocket. It read, 12:36.

"There's more than one move here, Kate." J.D. moved toward his bride. "And you going in there alone is the worst."

Kate shook her head. "It's the only way, J.D."

"How do you figure?"

"It gets us inside. Maybe I can figure what's happening out there and that'll help everyone. The Emma, Gentry, even Unity. Alabaster is a terrible man, J.D. I've looked in his eyes, touched him. There's an evil to him."

"That's why I don't want you going alone, Kate. We work best side-by-side. You and me. Hell, there's no guarantee they'll let Emma Wiley go anyway."

"I promised Emma we'd get to her husband, J.D. I promised it."

J.D. raised his hands. "I'm not saying we saddle the horses and ride away from here. I'm saying we do it the right way. Together."

Kate shook her head. "We need to get Emma away from Alabaster. He'll destroy her, J.D. She'll be perched in his brothel, broken and addicted, her only memory the torture that bastard bestowed on her."

J.D.'s blue eyes simmered, Kate could feel the anger and helplessness rise from him like an illness. She knew it wasn't something he felt often, and she didn't want him to feel it ever again. Still holding Joshua's hand, Kate motioned J.D. to her, pulled him close. Kissed his nose. An eye.

J.D. said, "You got a plan?"

Kate said, "No." Then released Joshua's hand and wrapped it behind J.D.'s neck. She pulled his mouth to hers and kissed him with urgency.

"I love you, J.D."

CHAPTER 21

It took less than an hour to dig Billy's grave. The service brief. Ames said a prayer that included several, "Our Heavenly Fathers," a plea for forgiveness—both for Billy and Ames—and not much about Billy's life. A nice service, but Kate hoped hers would be more conclusive about who she'd been, and maybe even why she'd been. And with luck, J.D. would be there mourning over her grave, so she wouldn't have to mourn over his.

Moon hugged Ames. His face shimmered silver with tears. "Billy would have enjoyed it."

J.D. nodded, took Kate's hand in his and squeezed gently.

The men went to work filling the hole. Kate moved towards the hotel, watched as several vultures circled above the valley where Guggenheim's man had fallen dead from Kate's bullet earlier in the day. She watched for several minutes before J.D. came to her side.

"Reckon we should do something with him?"

Kate shook her head. "I sure don't want to."

"Me either," J.D. said, "but it would be the Christian thing to do."

Kate looked at her husband sideways. "You're a philosopher now, are you?" She smiled to let him know it was a tease. "We'll bury him after we get Emma and Stephen away from Guggenheim."

J.D. nodded. "We need to be real careful tonight. I have no plans of planting you anytime soon."

"Or me, you." Kate pulled the train watch from her pocket. 4:19. "I better get ready."

The sun wound its way to the western horizon. Shadows stretched longer with each tick of the clock. An anxiousness enveloped the *Ames-Moon Stage Coach Inn* for the dangerous job ahead. No one said a word. J.D. and Joshua saddled four horses while Gentry, Ames and Kate watched from the hotel's porch.

Joshua brought Kate her horse. It whinnied nervously as she took the reins, seeming to understand the peril ahead. Kate patted its shoulder, cooed gently in its ear before placing her left foot in the stirrup, right hand on the saddle horn and without any obvious effort hoisted herself into the seat. The stillness such that she heard saddle leather creak, the jangle of spurs. She felt half-naked sitting the horse, her Colt and its holster missing from her hip and the scabbard gone from the saddle. Her only protection a three-inch blade buried in her left boot.

When she looked up all four men, everyone except Moon who was in the kitchen doing chores, stood shoulder to shoulder. J.D. and Ames with thumbs hooked in their belts, Joshua's shoulders slumped and Gentry grimacing.

"You're the glummest bunch I've ever seen." The thought of Billy kept Kate caught from comparing it to a funeral. In a light tone she continued, "I reckon you're either hungry or feeling bad about the only woman in ten miles riding off."

"I don't like this one damn bit," Gentry said. A sour look to his face.

His words burst a dam because everyone seemed to

speak at once.

Joshua said, "Please don't go Mrs. Kate."

"There's other ways, ma'am," James Ames said.

Kate nodded and tried to smile. She opened her mouth to speak, but closed it when no words came.

J.D. said to the men, "Once Kate's decided something there's no more arguing." He closed the distance between he and Kate and took her hand. A smile on his face. "It's not like we won't be seeing you in a few hours anyway."

Kate burst into laughter. J.D.'s easy manner silly, but welcome. "I better see you, big man, because if you have any plans to ride out for a better woman I'll hunt you all the way to your grave."

J.D.'s brow scrunched, showing his concern about the powder keg Kate was about to ignite. "It doesn't exist."

Kate tilted her head with confusion. "What doesn't exist?"

"A better woman."

Kate wanted to cry, but stifled it. Joshua giggled.

Gentry said, "I've sure never met one better. *Anyone* better for that matter."

Kate coughed politely into her hand, embarrassed by Gentry's words. "I'll see you at eight."

But before she could turn her horse away, Moses Moon appeared in the hotel's door. "Mrs. Blaze! A moment, please."

Kate held her ground. A questioning look on her face.

"I have something you'll want." The small man held an even smaller pistol towards her. A silver-plated two-shot over-under derringer. "It belonged to my late wife and I was afraid I wouldn't be able to find it."

Kate took the pistol from Moon and studied the fine engravings on its barrels for a moment. The black grips cool in her hand. She broke its chamber open and verified loads in each barrel. She bowed her head slightly and said, "Thank you, Moses."

"It'll shoot accurate to about ten feet." Moon pulled two small .22 caliber rounds from his pocket, handed them over. "I don't have any more."

Kate pushed the derringer into her right boot. The two extra rounds in her jeans' front pocket. She brought the horse around, pointed its head towards the Wiley's homestead. A few tears popped from Kate's eyes, her back to the men so they couldn't see, as she rode.

"Good luck, Mrs. Kate!" shouted Joshua.

Kate waved without turning around. A smile on her face at the boy's words. And for a moment she thought how easy it would be to keep him around.

CHAPTER 22

The flora changed from greasewood, sagebrush and juniper to ponderosa, quaking aspen and fir. The soil darkened to a rich brown as the trail moved steadily higher. In the distance Kate could see the ragged rocky peaks rising above the tree line, their eastern slopes stained orange by the dropping sun. The wilderness alive with chirping birds, unseen animals rustled in the underbrush. The clip-clop of Kate's shod horse. The air fresh and cool.

Kate didn't notice when the small noises disappeared and left her alone with nothing except her horse's clip-clopping. The beat of her heart.

"That's far enough."

An easy, calm voice broke the silence and startled Kate. She pulled her horse's reins back, a whinny and snort its response. The darkening forest at the trail's edge a mask to her eyes.

"I'm stopped," Kate said. Her hands clasped on the saddle's horn.

"You alone?"

Kate sighed. "Do you see anyone else?"

"What about it, Timmons? You see anybody else?"

Behind Kate, a horse clattered down a slope until it hit the trail with a clomp. Kate turned in her saddle to see a familiar man wearing a riverboat hat, a red vest under a dark waistcoat. It took her a moment to place him, but she sighed when she remembered the man heckling Sheriff Gentry when he arrested J.D. for killing Deputy Haskins.

"Nobody I saw."

"Timmons," Kate said.

The man sat the horse lazily and grinned like the devil as he urged the animal toward Kate. "That's me."

"You work at the *Wanderlust*?"

"Yes, ma'am." A mirthless laugh, high pitched and ugly. "That'll probably be the last time anyone calls you that."

"Ma'am?" Kate said.

"You'll be less than a lady when Guggenheim gets done with you."

"Promises, promises," Kate said. "The more a man boasts, the less satisfaction I seem to get."

"You're a peach, girlie. I understand why Guggenheim wants you." He pulled up a few feet shy of Kate. "Do you think Marcus will mind if I take a bite first, Sully?"

"Shut up."

Timmons raised both hands in surrender. To Kate he said, "I guess I'll have to wait my turn."

Kate smiled, an alluring curve to her lips. "I can't wait, Mr. Timmons."

She turned forward to see the man called Sully move onto the trail.

"You bring a gun?"

Kate shook her head. "I didn't think Alabaster would like that."

Sully smiled. "Alabaster? That's clever. If I were you I'd keep that name to myself, Mrs. Blaze."

Kate sat straight in the saddle. "Not sure I can keep it to myself, being clever and all. We sitting here, or we going somewhere?"

Sully stared at Kate for a few beats, nodded. He clicked his tongue against his check, turned his horse up trail, his back to Kate. "Sure, but I wouldn't think you'd be anxious to get there any sooner than you have to." He spurred his horse forward. "Don't let her shoot me in the back, Timmons."

The gambler chuckled. "That'd be a shame."

• • •

J.D. followed Ames closely. The landscape forbidding as it changed from desert to mountainous. The mesa and plateau far behind. They kept away from the trail as they circled toward Wiley's homestead. Behind him rode Gentry and Joshua. The boy's presence a secret since Kate was dead set on him staying at the *Ames-Moon*. But, J.D. figured, it was better to have the boy at his side than following somewhere out of sight.

Ames came to a stop and waved J.D. forward.

When J.D. came even, Ames said, "Wiley's place sits half a mile that way." James pointed to the north and east at a small depression covered by fir and quaking aspen, a short broken rock wall at its back.

J.D. said, "What's Wiley farming? Trees?"

Ames glanced at J.D., a smile on his face. "He is a city boy."

"I'm not sure anybody's so city they'd want to farm in those trees."

Gentry moved next to J.D. "That's not a farm."

J.D. nodded. "Where's Wiley's camp, James?"

Ames pointed to a spot at the depression's center. A little better than a hundred yards from the broken cliff. J.D. pulled a looking glass from a saddle bag, studied the area, but saw nothing except trees and rocks.

J.D. turned back to Ames. "You sure this is the place?"

"Sure as I can be."

"Okay." He turned in his saddle. "You two ready?"

Gentry and Joshua nodded.

J.D. said to Joshua, "You're with me, little man."

Ames put a hand on J.D.'s shoulder before he could ride away. "You think this is going to work?"

J.D. thought about Kate alone on the trail below. "Kate's probably about there. I'm not leaving without her."

"You ready, Ira?" Ames slapped his horse on the rump and started forward.

The lawman grunted and followed the hotelier as he rode to the left to curl behind the broken rock wall.

J.D. watched the pair ride for a few moments. He motioned to Joshua.

"You know this area?"

The boy nodded, his ever-present grin a little larger than normal.

"You ever seen Wiley's camp?"

Joshua thought for a moment. "No, but close once."

"Do you think you can get us there?"

Joshua sat so straight in his saddle, J.D. thought his spine might pop through his chest. His face stern with pride. "I can, Mr. J.D."

"Take us there," J.D. said.

CHAPTER 23

A canvas tent sat in a tiny clearing, surrounded by aspen. A tin chimney pipe at its back. The tent's flaps closed; pale yellow light illuminated its walls from within. A cracked shaving mirror hung against an aspen's nearly translucent bark and reflected sunset's hazy orange light. Two men stood by a campfire, mouths agape, and stared as the riders entered the camp.

Timmons hustled his horse next to Kate, a sneer on his face. "We're here."

"I hope there's somewhere for a girl to wash up." Kate smiled benignly.

Sully shouted, "We got her!"

Fifty yards into the trees a hooded man stepped from behind a ponderosa. "Good to have you, Mrs. Blaze."

Kate recognized the voice as Alabaster's. A tremor moved across her back, cold goosebumps prickled in its wake. Panic threatened to rise; hardened in her throat. She counted a few numbers, breathed consciously with every beat, watched as the hooded man delicately walked on his toes across the open ground.

"It's my pleasure." Her voice surprisingly strong. "Is there a masquerade party?"

Alabaster stopped, cocked his head. "You are a pistol, my dear Kate, but as a smart woman like you can surmise, my fair skin tends to chafe."

"Chafe?" Kate said. "I think you mean burn."

"I'm going to enjoy you, Kate. You're intelligent, beautiful, and so very willful. Breaking you will be my sincere pleasure." He rubbed his hands together with glee. Kate imagined a childish smile on his face, lust-filled eyes at the prospect of destroying another person.

"A marvelous goal. I imagine torturing yet another small animal must seem rather dull at this point in your life, Mr. Guggenheim. It's a shame, really." Kate paused for a moment, looked upwards as if contemplating her words.

"A shame?" Guggenheim said.

"You know," Kate looked to Timmons and Sully and back to the hooded man, "your inability to perform when your partner is warm and breathing. At least, I've heard you like it cold. Is that true?"

Timmons laughed; Sully looked uncomfortable.

Guggenheim remained silent. A slight tremor in his hands and arms.

A playful smile, a coquettish batting of eyelashes.

Alabaster, a faint crack in his voice, said, "This will be a pleasure."

"Where's Emma?" Kate's voice strong, a hard look on her face.

Sully looked from Kate to Guggenheim and back. A nervous twitch under his right eye. "She's in the tent."

"Shut your mouth!" Alabaster said to Sully.

Sully dropped his chin to his chest.

Alabaster closed the distance between he and Sully, put a finger in his face. "You speak when I tell you to speak, and not before."

Sully nodded.

To Kate, Alabaster said, "Good help is hard to find."

"Me for Emma, Mr. Guggenheim. That was the deal."

"You *are* a prize, Kate Blaze; beautiful, intelligent and naïve." Alabaster turned to Timmons, "Put her in the tent with the girl," and then he walked back to where he had come from.

Timmons dismounted. To Sully he said, "Take Buster."

Sully took the reins without a word, sulking from his rebuke.

"Get down," Timmons said to Kate.

Kate studied the fancy man for a moment and then looked at Sully. "They don't respect you, do they?"

Sully lifted his head, eyes blazing. "You don't know what you're talking about, lady."

Kate smiled. "You sound like a battered wife."

Sully growled, pivoted from his mount. He hit the ground with a grunt; looked at Timmons who watched the scene with folded arms. A grin on his face. An obvious enjoyment to his demeanor. Sully howled with rage and charged Kate.

Kate moved her horse forward a step and turned it sharply towards Sully. Its powerful haunch slammed against the attacking man with a meaty thud. Sully bounced backwards. His howl changed from rage to pain. He landed on his back, air whooshed from his mouth. His eyes bulged. Kate saw him struggle to breathe. She turned quickly towards Timmons with a plan to run him down, but instead she stared at a short-barreled Colt's large bore.

"That was fun, girlie, but you better come down off the horse or I'll shoot you."

Kate pulled back on the reins. She glared at Timmons and decided he had no qualms about pulling the trigger. She swiveled from the saddle and stood next to her horse. She puzzled at her predicament, calculated the odds of getting the derringer.

Timmons pointed at Kate's horse. "Step away, girlie."

She moved a few feet away from the horse, but no closer to Timmons or Sully, still lying on his back wheezing for breath.

"That's good, girlie." Timmons seemed to relax, but when Kate made a move to dodge behind a tree, hoping to gain enough time to palm the derringer hidden in her boot, the fancy man closed the distance in a blink. He brought the revolver's barrel down against the side of her head with a chopping motion.

Thunder rolled across Kate's vision, pain flared.

• • •

The rocky peaks high above greedily grasped the day's last moments as the valley drowned in darkness. J.D. paused to listen. Crickets chirped, mosquitos buzzed, small animals rustled from their burrows to hunt or be hunted. In the distance a hazy yellow-orange glow, a campfire kissing the night, marked the site where Kate should be. Where J.D. hoped Kate would be.

Joshua came even with J.D. and touched his hand in the darkness. When J.D. looked, the boy pointed to a narrow gap in the underbrush. "A game trail, Mr. J.D."

J.D. followed the boy to the slash of broken vegetation and followed it silently toward the campsite's light. A gentle night breeze tickled his face and whispered across the forest with creaking trees and fluttering leaves. J.D.'s nerves taut, his Colt heavy in his hand. His thoughts firmly on Kate.

CHAPTER 24

It started as a single band of pain. It wrapped itself around Kate's head from a great distance. A distraction at first, but pulling tighter second by second until her head felt like it would burst. Her vision black, white stars pulsed and then faded with each heartbeat. A droning buzz filled her ears and isolated her from the world she knew existed beyond this dark pool.

A sensation startled Kate. A gentle caress to her face, her head. A coolness doused the agony momentarily before being battered down by waves of nausea. She tried rolling onto her side, but the movement fragmented her skull.

She gasped. The muscles in her neck and shoulders contracted with rising panic. Her breathing irregular and harsh. Electric pain arced across her head and down her spine when she tried to rise. She fell back, eyes closed, terror mounting.

"It's okay." The whispered words calmed Kate. At first sounding unreal before becoming solid and unmoving in her mind. "You're fine, Kate. Please don't move."

Kate opened her eyes without understanding they had been closed. Her vision glazed and fuzzy before focusing on Emma's face. A shadowy smile touched the girl's mouth.

"I can see you," Emma said. "You're fine."

Kate forced herself still.

Emma massaged her face and scalp with a tender touch.

"Where am I?" Kate said.

"At the camp." Emma's voice disjointed from her lips.

Her memory flared. The fight with Timmons, the handgun's heavy impact on her skull. She sat up with Emma's help, closed her eyes and let the stars circle and fall. When the world stopped spinning, her eyes fluttered open.

She blinked at her soiled white surroundings. It took her a moment to realize she was in the tent. Its canvas walls and ceiling filthy.

A small bed at the back, a table with a bright lantern next to the door.

Kate looked up at the girl. "Why are you here, Emma?"

The girl said, "He came and took me."

"Guggenheim?"

Emma nodded, Kate heard her snuffle and felt a cold tear plop on her cheek.

"Is Mrs. Tiller hurt?"

"Yes."

"Bad?"

Emma shook her head. "I- I mean. He hit her, but she was breathing."

Kate nodded. "Okay. That's good. We'll check on her when we get back to Unity."

The girl went still. "Do you think—?"

Kate knew what the girl was asking. "We'll be in Unity before dawn, Emma."

"Safe?"

"Safe and sound," Kate said, "Do you think you can help me stand?"

Emma helped Kate to her feet. She wobbled a moment and then took a few small steps to test her strength. A smile on her face when she didn't fall. Kate wandered around the tent's interior before she stopped at the table and leaned against it for support.

"Where's your husband?"

The girl stared at her feet, with her fingers she worried at a loose thread in her dress.

"Emma? Is he hurt?"

The girl remained silent. A fat tear splattered on the dirt floor.

The tent's flap opened.

Kate jumped. She reached for where her Colt would normally be strapped to her hip and cursed its absence. She stepped away from the table to separate herself from the tent's door.

A bare-headed man ducked beneath the flaps, hat in hand. A light-colored waistcoat over a frilly city shirt. A wide forehead, close-set eyes. A gun strapped to his hip.

"Stephen?" Emma said.

He waved the girl off, looked at Kate. "I was told you were beautiful, Mrs. Blaze, but the descriptions failed you."

Kate looked to Emma and then back to Stephen Wiley. "I don't understand."

"I'm the bad guy." Stephen moved past Kate to Emma and reached for her hand. When she pulled away, he made a clicking noise with his tongue.

"You? You wanted Haskins to kill Emma?"

Stephen grimaced. "Deputy Haskins was to bring her here for an unfortunate accident. But his incompetency and your husband ruined it."

"Why?" Kate said.

"For this"—Stephen's arms went wide—"It all belongs to me when she dies, but not before. Her father didn't trust me for some reason."

Kate shook her head. "The land? It's worthless. The altitude makes farming impossible and if there was gold the Indian reservation wouldn't be here."

Stephen looked at his wife, grinned like a bastard. "No one sees your inheritance's promise, do they, darling?"

Kate said, "Why don't you tell me?"

Stephen glared at Kate with scorn. "You're as foolish as this," he pointed to Emma, "this twat."

"Stephen...please." Emma reached for the hand he had offered her a few minutes before, but he pulled it away. "I love you."

Wiley turned on his wife. An evil glint in his eyes. He yanked her closer by her hair, slapped her face, then threw her to the ground. "I've heard enough from you to last a lifetime."

Emma whimpered. Her eyes swimming with tears.

"You sicken me. The sight of you. Your body. The very idea that a stupid mouse like you could attract a man like me is ludicrous. You wormy little bitch." He turned on his heel and walked past Kate and exited the tent.

Kate kneeled next to Emma and pulled her close with an embrace. She caressed the girl's pale hair. Emma's head fell on Kate's shoulder. Her own pain forgotten as she comforted the girl. The two women stayed on the hard ground for several minutes, not moving. Kate said, "I'm sorry," over and over.

Emma's body racked with grief at her husband's betrayal. Her face covered with tears.

After a time, Kate helped Emma to the small cot at the tent's rear, where she rolled onto her side and curled into the fetal position.

As Kate stood from the bed, the door flap's familiar rustle caught her attention. When she turned, her breath caught in her throat, her heart lurched.

"There you are, my love. Stephen told me you were aroused."

"A sensation I'm sure you've never felt without blood on your hands." Kate's mouth a line, her eyes narrowed, and for the first time in her life she had murder in her heart.

CHAPTER 25

Ira Gentry's shoulder hurt like a bastard. His hand numb in the makeshift sling. His world reduced to a star brightened sky above and brooding thin boned ponderosa and fir everywhere else. His chest tight with claustrophobia from a lifetime spent on the plains past the eastern Rockies' foothills. Ahead, Ames moved with sure-footed grace. He paused infrequently to decide on the best path, like a man born to this rugged country.

The rangy hotelier came to a stop and signaled Gentry to join him. When the lawman was even with Ames he saw the cliff's edge. Below them, a meadow spread across the landscape. A campfire licked the sky with orange flames, dry wood popped and cracked and embers sparked high with the pine scented smoke.

The night buzzed with unabashed conversation and laughter. The words mostly indecipherable, but the few Gentry understood made him cold.

"The bastard really tears them up..." Kate's name in the mix, Emma's, too. The promise of wealth and whiskey bright on the men's tongues.

"I count three." Ames' eyes never left the campsite that stood some two hundred yards away.

A dozen feet from the fire, a tent glowed warmly. Elongated shadows from its inhabitants moved awkwardly along the walls.

Gentry said, "At least two in the tent."

"Where would they put Kate?"

Gentry shook his head. "She's not at the fire. In the tent? Emma, too?"

Ames said, "You reckon one of those men killed Billy?"

Gentry grunted without comment. He had heard murder on a man's voice before. He understood the emotion, but he couldn't condone the action no matter the circumstance. It was still murder even if the victim deserved a seat in hell, and he was certain these men had earned their tickets to the graveyard. But he was a lawman, and murder was murder no matter who did the killing and who did the dying.

He studied Ames' thin face for a moment without the man seeming to notice. His skin taut around the eyes and the mouth. His hat back on his head, his forehead crinkled with concentration. After several seconds Ames stood and moved along the cliff top until he found a narrow gash leading to the meadow below.

Ames paused and signaled Gentry to follow and dropped beneath the rock's surface and into the steep passage. Gentry close behind, studied the trail with unease. Its narrow floor littered with broken, crumbling shale. Its trajectory steep and unforgiving. The lawman looked at his arm sling. He sighed and stepped into the passage. The Colt in his left hand, the right strapped tightly at his chest.

He lost sight of Ames as he worked his way down the trail. The rocks slippery under his boots. He moved in inches, one foot and then the other. His left hand's heel on the jagged rock surface for balance. Every few feet he dislodged a rock to tumble down the sheer rock face. A cold fear crept into his stomach, tightened his chest. He felt old and scared for the first time in his life.

Then it happened.

His foot slipped on flat and loose shale.

He slid sideways and down. He jammed his left hand against the torn-up stone, the Colt clattered from his grasp, bounced and disappeared. His knuckles scraped across the jagged surface, pain peeled with his skin.

His balance gone, Gentry fell forward. He tried to raise his right arm, but the sling trapped it. He tumbled and slammed against the ground.

Molten agony blossomed from his gunshot wound. He grunted in fear and pain as he careened down the incline. An aspen tree halted his slide with a thump. The tree shuddered, Gentry's vision paled then darkened with confusion; throbbing painful waves kept him conscious. Alert.

He cursed.

Rocks avalanched behind him, smashed together, their rumble boomed across the night. A stunned silence fell across the meadow for two long heartbeats. Gentry searched the ground nearby for Kate's borrowed Colt as wild shouts and fast talk spread in the camp.

"You okay?" Ames whispered from below.

"Shit," Gentry responded.

A flame reached across the darkness, a shattering roar echoed. Gentry flattened, tried to disappear beneath the rocky soil.

The atmosphere electric with the bullet's passage.

• • •

J.D. and Joshua were inside the tree line at the meadow's edge when the night exploded.

A clatter of rock and whispered voices. An ear-splitting boom.

The muzzle flash yellow-white in J.D.'s peripheral vision. Its image burned stark against the night. Another shot followed, and then another.

J.D. processed their new situation. Their chance for surprise gone. Gentry and Ames in trouble across the meadow. With a split-second decision, he raised the Colt and aimed at the spot where the gunfire erupted and pulled the trigger. The .44 bucked pleasantly in his hand.

He moved deeper into the trees. Joshua a few feet behind. J.D. wanted separation from where he had taken the shot. He started away from the meadow and then moved parallel with it for several yards before he turned back towards the camp. At the tree line J.D. stepped behind a large aspen, ejected the spent shells from the Colt's cylinder and replaced each with a fresh round. When he was fully loaded, J.D. turned to Joshua. The boy lying prone. The Winchester's barrel on a stump as he looked for targets.

"Stay here. And don't shoot me!"

J.D. moved hesitantly into the meadow. The men in disarray, heads down. He straightened and ran at full speed when he realized the confusion would make it easy to breach the camp's perimeter without much fuss from the bad guys. The uneven ground hard and unforgiving. The tent directly ahead.

The tent's front flap rattled. Naked light spilled out.

J.D. dropped to the ground. He rolled behind a rotting tree fallen long ago. The Colt in his hand. A ghost, pale and ugly appeared in the tent's doorway. Fear and determination on his face. The devil himself, J.D. thought. The albino.

J.D. sighted the Colt's barrel at the ugly man, pulled the trigger.

The man lurched, ducked low and ran along the tent toward the back of the meadow. J.D. cursed at the missed opportunity. He fired at the man's retreating figure with the same result. The albino disappeared around the tent.

J.D. sighed, wiped sweat from his brow. He stood on bent knees and eased closer to the tent. The men at the campfire gained some respectability as the albino shouted orders. A few wild shots echoed in the night. A shower of dirt erupted to J.D.'s right. Then from outside the camp a rifle boomed. The campfire men dropped to the ground, their rifles silent.

J.D. crawled to the tent's blank canvas door on hands and knees. The shadowy dance from earlier now gone.

J.D. whispered, "Kate."

A commotion from within the tent, without a verbal response to his inquiry, gave J.D. the idea Kate wasn't in the tent or she didn't know it was him.

So he tried again. "Kate. It's me, J.D.!"

• • •

Dirt rained across Gentry's back. With his free hand, he searched for the lost Colt.

When he felt its cold steel with a finger he wanted to exclaim, but instead he palmed the big gun and scooted backwards on his belly. The dirt and rocks scratched his face. The pain in his shoulder forgotten as an unseen shooter attempted to ventilate him a second time in a single day. He hit a short rock wall at the narrow passage's edge. He sat up and slid feet first to the cliff's base. A sense of relief when he found ankle high grass. And more relief when he was behind a large split boulder.

Gentry took a snap shot at his tormentor. The gun bucked awkwardly in his left hand. He wasn't much of a pistol shot on his best day, but with his weak hand he was hopeless.

He turned to the camp. The three campfire men moved in upset circles. He spotted Ames' shadow for a moment before it disappeared into the undergrowth ahead.

After several seconds, Ames popped up again. A dark oval against the fire's brightness. A lick of flame. A clap of thunder. The hotelier's rifle shouted at the night.

The nearest campfire man jerked. He landed on his back, skidded to the fire's edge. His face skyward. A leg twitched, fell motionless. Gentry hoped it was the son of a bitch who'd killed Billy.

A shadow moved across the illuminated tent to Gentry's right. A tall man. A crooked bowler on his head. A larger revolver in his hand. He shouted at the two surviving campfire men. The men calmed and took cover behind the sitting log at the fire's edge. No one appeared to notice their fallen comrade.

Another shot erupted from the tent's front side. The bullet's trajectory carried it several yards to Gentry's left. Its stomach-dropping crackle audible in his ears.

Gentry ducked. Cursed at the shooter.

The running man didn't flinch. He never looked back. He moved along the tent's side, skittered behind it to take away the shooter's angle and made a wide loop around the meadow.

Gentry recognized the man's gait as Guggenheim. The smarmy bastard moved like a man who knew what he was doing and where he was going. He raised the Colt, placed its bead on the albino.

His hand shook.

He didn't breathe.

Panic rose in his chest.

The lawman pulled his finger from the Colt's trigger as

fear crawled cold across him. He shouted at the night. At his impotence. His fear.

Guggenheim circled behind where Ames was hidden in the long grass. The hotelier unaware of the outlaw's approach.

The albino raised his pistol.

Gentry shouted, "James!"

Guggenheim fired at point blank range. Once. Twice.

Thunder rolled.

CHAPTER 26

When the shooting started Kate dropped to the tent's dirt floor.

Emma whimpered.

Alabaster grinned; madness sparkled in his pink eyes. Without a word he darted from the tent into gunfire.

Kate yanked her trouser leg above her boot and removed the derringer. She crawled to where Emma huddled on the cot. Kate motioned for the girl to silence with a finger to her lips. She grasped Emma's hand and squeezed reassuringly.

From outside J.D. whispered, "Kate."

Emma's eyes bulged with panic.

"Kate. It's me, J.D.!"

"I know who you are, J.D.!" Kate shouted. "Give me a second."

The tent's door flap pushed inward. J.D.'s grim face appeared. He moved on all fours to Kate and Emma.

"You okay?"

"You sure took your damn time getting here." Kate's relief at J.D.'s presence palpable in her tone if not her words. She turned back to Emma, said, "We need to get—"

The tent's door flap whisked open. Kate's and J.D.'s guns steady on the newcomer.

"Joshua?" Kate looked from the boy to J.D. "What's he doing here?"

"I told you to stay put." J.D. seemed determined to keep his eyes away from Kate's.

The Winchester in Joshua's hands. "I thought you needed help."

Kate shook her head. "We need to get out of here."

Joshua scurried to the back of the tent. He helped Emma to her feet, held her arm as they moved to the tent's door. Emma limped lightly on her hurt ankle. Kate watched the boy's bravery with pride. When he flinched and stopped she feared he had been shot, but his eyes were locked on an old parchment on the table.

Kate said, "What is it?"

A fat tear dropped to the dirt floor at Joshua's feet. He held his hand two inches above the parchment for a beat. Then lifted it from the table. A small yellowed newspaper clipping fluttered to the floor.

Kate placed her hand on the boy's shoulder. "Joshua?"

Joshua showed the parchment to her. A rough map drawn on its face. She looked from the boy to J.D., confusion in her eyes. "I don't understand."

J.D. passed the newspaper clipping to Kate. "This may help."

Kate read its first line, "Itinerant man found mutilated on West Broadway." To Joshua, she said, "Did you know this man?"

He looked at Kate with tear filled eyes. He nodded, motioned to the map. "This was my uncle's."

"Sonuvabitch," J.D. said.

The tent's interior faded to black when Kate turned off the oil lamp. Emma whimpered quietly, Joshua snuffled faintly.

"Joshua, take Emma into the trees and hide."

Kate turned to J.D. "We have work."

• • •

Gentry closed his eyes.

He cursed his injured arm and his new-found cowardice.

When he opened his eyes again, he saw Guggenheim standing over Ames' hiding place. The albino crouched down. A ghoulish smile on his shadowy face, an evil clown. He said a few words Gentry couldn't hear and then stood. He pointed his gun at Ames again.

Gentry fought panic. He stubbornly held the Colt. He aligned its front sight on Guggenheim's chest. His hand shaky and weak. He pulled the trigger.

The big revolver almost jumped from Gentry's hand; smoke and fire belched into the night.

Guggenheim staggered. He looked startled. His head swiveled from left to right.

Gentry started to pull the Colt's hammer back.

But Guggenheim bolted. He ran smoothly past the campfire. He disappeared into the trees at the meadow's far side.

Gentry took a deep breath. He counted his thundering heartbeats. At fifty, the lawman stood. His knees rubber. His bowels liquid. A hesitant step and then another moved him past the boulder and into the meadow.

His eyes alert, the Colt surprisingly steady in his left hand, he walked through the tender grass. A few feet shy of Ames' unmoving body, he stopped. He wiped sweat from his brow.

Gentry said, "Goddamn. I'm sorry, James."

• • •

J.D. eased from the tent. He held its flap open for Joshua and Emma. The two moved past him. Their only sounds were Emma's breathing and the swish of grass on feet and ankles.

Kate followed. She touched J.D.'s shoulder as she crossed through the door and pointed to the campfire where the men cowered behind their makeshift cover.

"We need to take care of those two."

J.D. motioned Kate to the left and he went to the right. No need for stealth since the men's faces were flush with the ground, mouths and noses buried in dirt. The night had fallen into eerie quiet. The soughing wind pushed trees, whispered through grass. The crack and pop of dry pine.

J.D. crouched down. He worked his way behind the men. Their backs to him. He moved silently, kept to his toes. When he was in position a few yards behind the men, J.D. checked on Kate. She stood twelve feet away. A 45-degree angle from J.D.

J.D. scowled when he realized her only weapon was the tiny derringer, but admired the woman's moxie. He knew Kate would face the devil, nothing but a .22 caliber double shot in her hand.

J.D. caught her eye. She nodded. He took a step forward. He raised the Colt to shoulder level. "Game's up, boys!"

Kate said, "Drop your guns!"

"Don't shoot!" The man nearest Kate threw his revolver in the air. It bounced a few feet from Kate. The man rolled over. A white streak in his hair and buck teeth in his mouth.

The other man held his gun up. His nose still in the dirt.

J.D. said, "Throw it away!"

When the man had obeyed, Kate retrieved the first gun and J.D. grabbed the other.

The Colt's dilapidation made J.D. think these two were far from hired guns.

Kate scowled at her new revolver. After a moment, she stuffed it in her belt. The derringer still in her right hand.

Kate said, "What are you boys doing here?"

Buck Teeth looked at her, more than simple confusion in his eyes.

"Well?" J.D. said.

He stammered, finally said, "We was hired to carry it." He looked at his companion, whose face was still in the dirt. "Ain't that right, Ennis?"

"That's right, Enos."

"Carry what?" J.D. said.

Buck Teeth—named Enos—looked at J.D with dull eyes. "The gold, mister. Ain't you here for the gold?"

"Where is it?"

The man with his face in the dirt. Ennis to his friends, it seemed. Pointed to a narrow trail. Its grass freshly flattened. "Over there."

Kate said, "You have a surname, Enos and Ennis?"

"A wha—"

"Slaughter, ma'am," Ennis said without lifting his face from the dirt.

J.D. said, "If we ever see you boys again, we'll kill you both."

Ennis lifted his head. He looked at his brother. "That mean we can go?"

"If you don't hurry it up, we'll shoot just because," J.D. said.

The brothers jumped to their feet, hollered at each other and ran into the trees.

"You think their parents were siblings?" Kate said.

"Siblings?"

"You know, brother and sister?"

J.D. grinned.

Kate looked at the dead man. "I know this one."

"Me too," J.D. said. "His name's Sully."

• • •

A shouted voice at the campfire startled Gentry. A grudging smile creased his face when he saw J.D. and Kate. Their guns raised against the two remaining campfire men. It gave him reassurance. A little of the courage taken by his gunshot wound and the day's pain seeped back into his body. He crouched next to Ames and took his pulse. The vein thudded strongly beneath his finger.

He turned James onto his back.

The hotelier's eyes fluttered open. A grim smile on his face. A bullet score on his left temple. James pointed to his ears and damn near shouted, "I can't hear nothing!"

Gentry put a finger to his lips. He smiled in what he hoped was a reassuring fashion. He sat back on his haunches, removed his arm from the sling and stretched it away from his body. He grimaced with pain.

"Can you stand?"

Ames squinted at Gentry's mouth, trying to decipher the words.

Gentry made a walking motion with his fingers.

Ames smiled. "Sure."

Gentry gave Ames a hand to his feet. He helped him walk to the where J.D. and Kate stood over the man Ames had killed.

Gentry said, "Am I glad to see you two."

• • •

J.D. pivoted at the voice. His Colt steady. Its barrel at the lawman's chest. He smiled when he recognized Ames and Gentry.

"I wondered when you two would show up."

Kate moved to the injured men. She took Ames' arm in her hand. She helped him to the fire where he sat on the ground. His back to the log where the Slaughter brothers had cowered only moments before.

"What happened?"

Gentry said, "Guggenheim creased him."

J.D. jerked at the albino's name. "Where is he?"

Gentry pointed to a narrow path leading into the forest. It was the same trail the Slaughters claimed led to gold. "Right down there."

J.D. looked at Kate. "Let's go."

"Hold up!" Gentry shouted. He held Kate's Colt by its barrel. "You'll need this."

CHAPTER 27

The starry shroud covered the valley so close Kate thought she could touch it if she tried. The night quiet as the grave. The trail moved from the meadow to the trees. It climbed several hundred feet before it dropped into another valley. This one smaller than the last. A light shimmered ahead. It was attached to what appeared to be a mine entrance. Heavy wooden braces at the edges and across the top. A doorway into the mountain's heart.

Three men talked animatedly in the mining lamp's flickering glow. Alabaster, Timmons and Wiley. Their words indistinct. Kate moved smoothly from the narrow path into the towering firs and ponderosas at its edge. The Colt comfortable in her hand. J.D. followed.

Kate's and J.D.'s approach slowed, but the men's distraction allowed them to move within several feet of the mine's entrance. Kate held her hand in the air to stop J.D.

"—as much mine as it is yours." Timmons poked Guggenheim's chest with an extended finger. The rhythm matched the cadence of his words. His face bright with anger, spittle splashed from his mouth.

Guggenheim stood his ground. His face taut with anger. He slapped Timmons' hand away.

Stephen Wiley stepped between the two men. A hand on each man's chest. He pulled his hand away from

Guggenheim. The palm level with the ground and gave him a "calm down" motion.

Guggenheim nodded. He took a small step back.

Wiley, his hand still on Timmons' chest, said, "We have a thousand gold bars"—he pointed to the mine entrance—"that's worthless if we take it to a bank like we found it. Its Spanish markings will set alarm bells off all over the territory. The tribe knows it's here. You understand that, right? The old man in Salt Lake lived out here on the reservation. He knew where it was, and others do, too. The feds will take it away if we try to cash it. The Utes will kill us if they find out we have it."

Timmons gulped. His face blanched pale in the lamp's light. "What about the Blazes?"

"We'll take care of them," Wiley said. "Just like we took care of Jones."

A careless smile rose on Timmons' lips. "He really made that rope jump, now, didn't he?"

Wiley returned the smile. "He sure did. We okay, now? You understand we need to keep our heads?"

Timmons, his eyes flat, nodded. "Yeah. Okay."

Wiley turned to Guggenheim. "We good?"

Guggenheim stood still for a moment, starring through Wiley, before he shoved him. Wiley stumbled backwards, slammed against the support beam to the mine's entrance, gasped as the air was forced from his lungs.

With his right hand Guggenheim pulled the fancy hog leg from its holster and shot the gambler between the eyes.

Timmons' blood misted a halo around the timid light, splattered in thick gobs on the mine entrance's cross beam. He crumpled in a heap, dead before he hit the ground.

"Holy—"

"Shut up!" Guggenheim shouted. "I'll shoot you if you

don't shut up."

Wiley stared at Alabaster, fear plain in his eyes.

Kate looked over her shoulder at J.D. Then she stepped onto the narrow trail. The Colt at shoulder level. Its barrel pointed straight at Guggenheim. Who stood less than ten feet away.

Kate said, "Drop it!"

Guggenheim visibly flinched, his fingers loose on the gun. He turned his head a few inches towards Kate.

"Do what the lady said." J.D. was at Kate's right shoulder. His big Colt ready.

Kate grinned. "This is the husband I told you about."

Guggenheim seemed to grow paler when he saw the two gunnies. He looked at his silver-plated revolver. He hefted it in the palm of his hand as if he were seeking its guidance.

"I wouldn't, Guggenheim," J.D. said, "Kate's looking for an excuse to plant you."

Alabaster smiled, raised his pistol.

Kate's first shot hit Guggenheim in the chest. The second caught him below the left eye. The albino stood straight. His hands at his sides. The gun dropped from his fingers. The smile plastered on his ugly face, blood blossomed from his mouth. He raised his right foot as if he were walking, but instead fell hard to the ground.

Stephen Wiley, his hands above his head, squealed.

Kate said, "I don't like agreeing with Guggenheim, but if you don't shut up, I'm going to shoot you."

The city man's face pale. His eyes wide, closed his mouth.

"Her bark's worse than her bite," J.D. said.

Wiley looked at Guggenheim's dead body, then at J.D. He opened his mouth to talk or scream, but thought better of it.

"You boys found some Spanish gold on Indian ground, I take it?" J.D. said. His Colt back in its holster.

Wiley nodded.

"You were going to move it to Wiley's land, melt it down and pass it off as fresh ore? That's what you boys had planned?"

Wiley sat silent. His face pale, shock in his eyes.

Kate said, "You get the idea from the Ute you killed in Salt Lake?"

Wiley looked at J.D.

"Don't you look at him for help."

J.D. held his hands up in a helpless gesture. "I'd answer, if it was me looking at a .44's bad end in Kate Blaze's steady hands."

"It was Guggenheim's idea. All of it."

"I bet," Kate said. "You kill the Indian?"

Wiley shook his head.

Kate said, "I bet you're going to tell us Alabaster did the deed, right?"

"That's right." His voice a whisper.

"What about Emma's dad?"

Wiley blinked. He looked from Kate to J.D. and back.

Kate said, "Why'd you kill him?"

"I. I—"

"Hold it," J.D. said. "You better save it for your wife. She'll want to know why you killed her father."

"I want to shoot him, J.D."

J.D. glanced at his wife. "Then we'd have to haul his sorry ass out of here. Better we make him walk and let Gentry hang him in a week or two."

Kate glared, but lowered the Colt.

J.D. said, "How'd you know they killed Emma's dad?"

Kate grimaced. "Lucky guess."

J.D. laughed, changed the subject. "This is what I call an anniversary, Kate. Murder, gold and land grabs."

Kate shook her head. "You owe me big for this one. It's my turn tonight and I'm not going to bathe."

J.D. looked glum. "No bath? After I gave you that necklace and everything?"

Kate smiled. "Last night was your present."

Then, "And I'm not bathing tonight."

BLAZE!
The All-New Adult Western Series

J.D. and Kate Blaze are two of the deadliest gunfighters the Old West has ever seen. They also happen to be husband and wife, as passionate in their love for each other as they are in their quest for justice on the violent frontier!

BLAZE! by Stephen Mertz

BLAZE! #2: THE DEADLY GUNS by Robert J. Randisi

BLAZE! #3: BITTER VALLEY by Wayne D. Dundee

BLAZE! #4: SIX-GUN WEDDING by Jackson Lowry

BLAZE! #5: AMBUSHED by Michael Newton

BLAZE #6: ZOMBIES OVER YONDER by Stephen Mertz

BLAZE #7 HATCHET MEN by Michael Newton

**BLAZE! #8: RIDE HARD, SHOOT FAST by Wayne D.

Dundee

BLAZE #9: A SON OF THE GUN by Stephen Mertz

BLAZE #10: HELL'S HALF ACRE by Jackson Lowry

BLAZE! #11: BADLANDS by Michael Newton

BLAZE! #12 BLOODY WYOMING by John Hegenberger

BLAZE! #13 NIGHT RIDERS by Michael Newton

BLAZE! SPECIAL HOLIDAY EDITION: THE CHRISTMAS JOURNEY by Stephen Mertz

BLAZE! #15: RED ROCK RAMPAGE by Ben Boulden

BLAZE! #16 COPPER MOUNTAIN KILL by Brian Drake

BLAZE! #17 BAD MEDICINE by Michale Newton

BLAZE! #18: SPANISH GOLD by Ben Boulden

Made in the USA
Columbia, SC
20 October 2023